TASKFORCE
THE BUG WARS
ERIC S BROWN

SEVERED PRESS
HOBART TASMANIA

TASKFORCE THE BUGWARS

ISBN: 978-1-925493-76-4

THE BUG WARS

Marcus Page yawned, reclining in his chair at the long-range sensor station. Normally, he loved the night shift. This evening though, he was having trouble staying awake. Two cups of coffee had helped, but they weren't fully doing the job. His third sat on the console of his station, half drained. There was never that much traffic around Cerebus VI anyway, and at night, the entire system was usually a dead zone.

Cerebus VI was on the very edge of Solar Federation space. Its colony was a small one by Solar Federation standards. The total population of Cerebus VI was a mere three hundred million people. Most of them were farmers or miners by trade. Cerebus VI only had two commodities that made it of value to the Solar Federation: its exported crops and its orbital shipyards. Three years ago, the planet's conservative party had come to power politically and cut a deal with Earth Gov. that made Cerebus VI one of the Solar Federation's most up-and-coming builders of ships. The planet's vast resources in terms of subsurface metals, and its location at the edge of Solar Federation space, had given it an edge in landing the deal to become one of the top producers of explorer class vessels. Marcus had voted more on the liberal side but in the end had been glad that the conservatives had won. Cerebus VI was booming in terms of industry now compared to where it had been as solely a food-producing world back then.

He had graduated from a two-year course at the new space academy and had been able to escape what otherwise would have been his inevitable fate in becoming a farmer like his dad. Instead of breaking his back tending fields, he got to sit in a comfy chair, drinking coffee, and monitoring the in-and-out going ship traffic of the Cerebus system. For the most part, the job was easy and sometimes even fun. Only two times a year did it get harrowing. That was when the fleet of completed vessels were being crewed and dispatched into the great void of space beyond the Solar Federation's borders and when the harvests came in. Harvest time was the worst. Dozens of ships a day would come into the system to pick up their hauls, and an almost equal number of small-time dealers would launch their own freighters from the planet's spaceports packed hull to hull with carrots, potatoes, etc. Old Earth foods truly flourished in the soil of Cerebus IV, and the demand for them was always high; the Earth herself was the center of power for the Solar Federation now and the bulk of her surface was either industrialized or used for defensive military purposes.

Struggling to keep his eyes open and stay alert, Marcus rocked forward in his chair reaching for his coffee. He should have spent the day sleeping like he usually did but Gwen had asked him to spend it with her. No sane human male would turn down the chance to spend time with a young woman like Gwen. She was smoking hot, full of energy, and the epitome of adventurous. She had booked a shuttle to Cerebus VI's surface for the two of them and taken him to eat at Rancheros, one of the premier burger spots on the planet. The joint was located in her hometown where she had grown up, so after their meal, she had dragged him to go skinny-dipping in a swimming hole near her old home. One thing led to another and well... Marcus was surprised he was still conscious at all if the truth be told.

Orbital Defense Platform Alpha didn't have much of a crew or a bridge to speak of. Most of its space was devoted to the massive array of armaments the platform boasted. Its living quarters were even smaller than its bridge and rather cramped, Spartan rooms. Regulations required a permanent onboard crew of four with a rotating staff of up to six additional crew members who stayed aboard from a couple of days to a few weeks at a time depending on their specialty and their rank. Marcus was one of the permanent crewmembers, so getting the day off for Gwen hadn't been easy. He had to move heaven and earth to do so, but it had been oh so worth it.

The chronometer on his station read 2:44 AM. That meant he had another four hours and sixteen minutes until the day crew showed up to relieve him of duty. Since this was the slow season, he was the only person on the bridge tonight and time was dragging by like sap dripping from a tree in winter. He fiddled with the bridge's environmental controls lowering the temperature in hopes that the cold would help him stay awake since his coffee wasn't doing its job. He sighed and turned his thoughts to Gwen again and the curves of her body beneath the water. A smile stretched across his lips at the memory so fresh in his mind.

Most Orbital Defense Platform Alpha's systems were automated. They handled most ordinary occurrences on their own only alerting the human personnel if system traffic got heavy or something anomalous happened. Marcus almost spat out the mouthful of coffee he had been in the process of swallowing as he saw the red lights flashing on the console in front of him. He jerked himself upright in his chair, sitting down his coffee with so roughly that he nearly broke his favorite mug.

Something was up. The red lights meant that there was an unscheduled jump point opening in the Cerebus system. Marcus's fingers danced hurriedly over the keys on his console, pulling up the data he needed to confirm that jump point was truly unscheduled and not merely the arrival of an inbound ship that had gotten lost in the shuffle of orders and paperwork. Whoever was entering the system, they weren't on any of the lists. There weren't even any listed ships that looked to be capable of arriving this early. Sometimes ships did enter the Cerebus system earlier than planned, but those were rare events.

Marcus was in a panic as he called up the data on the jump point itself. It was massive. Inside the Cerebus system, there were Cerebus VI's three shipyards, the largest of which was the Endeavor, the ring of six defense platforms in orbit around the planet, and currently two patrol ships, both of which were far away from where the jump point was forming. The jump point was several times larger than the Endeavor which was utterly insane. The sprawling mass of the Endeavor contained not only the central heart of the shipyard but the extending structures that contained five Explorer class ships under construction. According to Marcus's data, the jump point was large enough to fit three shipyards the Endeavor's size into it easily with space to spare. He blinked as that information sunk in and quickly rechecked it. The data was spot on and correct.

Stabbing the button that activated Defense Platform Alpha's emergency klaxons, Marcus knew that this was all way beyond him. He needed Commander Threshal on the bridge as soon as possible. The bridge's lighting shifted from its normal sharp, brightness to a dim red as the platform went into alert status. The alarm klaxons blared throughout it. Marcus shut off the ones on the bridge and refocused his attention on the forming jump point calling up a visual of it. It looked like a giant purple tear in space blocking the view of the stars behind it. So far, nothing had emerged from it.

Marcus heard the lift doors swish open behind him as Commander Threshal and her first officer, Mikal, strode onto the bridge.

"Report!" Threshal snapped at him.

"Ma'am, unscheduled jump point has formed in Sector Beta. It's massive. Unlike anything I have ever seen before. So far nothing has emerged from it but..." Marcus stammered.

"Have you tried hailing any vessels that might be on the other side of the jump point?" Mikal cut in.

"Not yet, sir," Marcus said. pretending that he had thought of that himself, "I was just about to do so when you arrived."

"Do it now," Commander Threshal ordered.

"Sending standard jump point entry message, all languages and frequencies," Marcus told her as he worked.

After a second, he added, "No reply, ma'am."

"The weapons powered up as soon as the platform went to alert status," Mikal commented. "Let's hope we don't need them."

"Are we the only ones seeing this?" Commander Threshal asked.

"I don't see how we could be," Mikal answered before Marcus responded as he stared at the visual of the jump point Marcus had on the bridge's main screen. "Everyone in system has to be detecting that thing by now. Marcus wasn't kidding when he said it was massive." Mikal gave Marcus a nod.

"Defense Platforms Gamma and Obsilon have also gone to alert status, ma'am," Marcus confirmed. "Our two patrol vessels in system have also altered course to approach the jump point. The *Hagel* should reach it first given their respective positions. ETA in five."

"Alert the folks planet-side about what's happening up here, Marcus," Commander Threshal told him.

"Yes, ma'am." Marcus fought the urge to salute. He wasn't used to the platform's commander showing up to stand beside his station during the nightshift.

"Nothing we can do now but wait for whoever is out there to show their selves," Mikal said.

"Something tells me that we won't be waiting long." Commander Threshal continued to watch the forward screen as energy crackled around the edges of the warp point.

"Ships coming through!" Marcus reported.

Several formations of what appeared to be small destroyers emerged from the warp point. Each formation included three ships, one in the center with the other two flanking it. It was clear that the ships were military in nature and not just the normal civilian freighters that traveled into the Cerebus system.

"What are those?" Mikal muttered. "I've never seen anything like them."

"The platform's database hasn't either," Marcus added.

"We need to treat this as first contact scenario," Commander Threshal ordered. "There's no evidence, yet, that those unknowns are hostile."

More and more ships were emerging from the jump point. There were at least a dozen squadrons of destroyers in the system now.

"The *Hagel* is approaching the outlying wave of unknown vessels now," Marcus informed Commander Threshal. Most of the ships that had come through the warp point had taken up defensive positions surrounding it. Only one trio of destroyers had continued to move deeper into the system. According to Marcus's data, it was on an intercept course for the *Hagel*.

Commander Threshal reached around Marcus to open a channel to the patrol ship himself. "Captain Rucka, this is Commander Threshal aboard Defense Platform Alpha."

"Ma'am," Captain Rucka acknowledged her hail.

"These ships are of unknown origin and their intentions are questionable at best. Nonetheless, we need to avoid starting a confrontation if possible. Is that clear?"

"Yes, ma'am," Rucka said. "The *Hagel* is running hot, shields up and weapons readied, but we've made no move to target any of the unknown vessels."

"Good," Commander Threshal said. "Do not fire until fired upon."

Marcus frowned, knowing that the commander's order was a death sentence for Rucka and his crew if the aliens did prove hostile. One lone patrol ship couldn't possibly hope to survive the combined firepower of three destroyers unless the alien's tech level was far inferior to that of the Solar Federation. And from the size of the jump point the aliens had opened, that was a highly unlikely proposition.

If the ships in the wedge-shaped formations were truly destroyers, they moved about chunkily compared to their Solar Federation counterparts. They were also smaller. Their hulls appeared to be heavily armed, however. That could mean their shield tech was lacking, or it could simply mean that their race was one that thrived on war and such additional armor was standard for their vessels. If the aliens were a race that thrived on war, Cerebus VI was in some serious trouble.

"Mother of the Holy!" Mikal cried out, calling Marcus's attention back to the bridge's forward screen.

Another ship was emerging from the jump point. It was easily twice the size of the Endeavor shipyard and resembled something out of the worst kind of nightmare. Missile tubes covered its hull, concentrated on its bow but also running along the entire lengths of its sides. Large spikes protruded from its hull at random intervals. Marcus had no idea what purpose the things served, but they certainly added to the gigantic ship's already fearsome appearance.

The *Hagel* was now close enough to the trio of alien destroyers that had broken off from the main body of alien ships gathered around the warp point that it had slowed and brought itself to a dead stop in space. The three destroyers it faced had halted as well, as if they were staring down the *Hagel* and waiting on the patrol ship to make the first move.

The *Pinket,* the other patrol ship in the system, was closing fast on the *Hagel*'s position. Though the patrol ships really weren't much smaller than the three alien destroyers, they seemed fragile and extremely outmatched to Marcus.

"Maybe we should have gone on the offensive when we had the chance," Mikal said.

Commander Threshal snorted. "We never had the chance and you know it."

Marcus noticed a comm. signal coming through on his screen. "The aliens are transmitting something, ma'am."

Commander Threshal stared at him waiting for him to continue.

"The platform's translator software is unable to make any sense of it, ma'am. The aliens are transmitting it on all frequencies, though," Marcus told her.

"Frag it!" Commander Threshal was growing frustrated. "This could be our only chance to talk with them before they do open fire."

Marcus frowned as the transmission came to an end. Moments later, Marcus detected large power surges aboard the three destroyers facing down the *Hagel* and the *Pinket*. The alien ships were bringing their weapons online.

"This is Defense Platform Alpha," Commander Threshal screamed over the comm. to the patrol ships. "Get out of there now!"

The engines of the two patrol ships spiked in power as their captains tried to bring them about and make a run for Cerebus VI. As they did so, the three alien destroyers opened fire on them. The patrol ships and the alien destroyers were within beam weapon range of one another. Energy danced along the spikes of the alien ships, coalescing into bolts that blasted outwards at the retreating Solar Federation vessels. The *Hagel*'s shields pulsed blue as the bolts struck it. They held less than twenty seconds before they flickered out of existence, and the sustained fire of the alien vessel slashed a long groove along her side. Atmosphere vented into space from the *Hagel*'s deep wound. A second barrage of energy beams ripped into her from another of the alien vessels. This time, there were no shields to dampen the amount of damage the beams did. They must have struck something vital because the *Hagel* erupted into a blossoming ball of orange fire. Debris spun away from the explosion as she died instantly.

The *Pinket* was lucky. She was further away from the trio of enemy ships and only one of them attacked her. Its energy beams raked across her stern, but her shields held long enough for her initiate evasive maneuvers. She went into a roll, twisting out of the alien ship's line of fire as she continued to build up speed.

"She's not going to make it," Mikal commented.

"Let's see that she does," Commander Threshal said. "Marcus, lock onto those alien ships and let them know that we're here."

Marcus didn't smile. He knew that as powerful as the orbital defense platforms around Cerebus VI were, they, too, didn't stand a chance against the amount of enemy ships already in the system, much less anything else that came through the gigantic warp point.

"Yes, ma'am," Marcus answered, "Targets acquired."

He stabbed a button on his console. "Missiles away. ETA- two minutes."

Commander Threshal, Mikal, and Marcus watched the missiles as they closed on the alien ships. The *Pinket* continued to make a desperate run for the planet. So far, her luck was holding. The trio of alien ships had only taken a few additional pop-shots at her. It was as if they were playing with her, knowing they could end the chase at any moment of their choosing.

Marcus noticed new data scrolling across his personal screen. "Commander, the large alien vessel is powering up its weapons!"

Commander Threshal slammed a balled-up fist into the wall of the bridge. He didn't need to ask what the large vessel was targeting. All three of them already knew. It didn't take a genius to figure it out.

The large alien vessel spat volleys of missiles, each hundreds strong, towards the shipyards of the Cerebus VI system. They streaked across the void towards their targets.

"The Endeavor is launching her fighters, ma'am," Marcus almost shouted, his emotions caught somewhere between excitement and sheer panic.

"It won't be enough to save her." Commander Threshal frowned, leaning over Marcus's shoulder to read the available data on the missiles approaching the shipyard. "There's too many of them and she launched too late."

As the Endeavor's fighters rushed to intercept the inbound missiles, the missiles that Defense Platform Alpha had launched reached the trio of alien ships pursuing the *Pinket*. Marcus had spread out the missiles among the three ships. Twelve targeted each of them. The lead alien ship's shields flashed as the missiles collided with it. Missile after missile hammered them. By the time all twelve missiles had expended themselves, the alien ship's shields were down and one of the missiles had torn away a solid chunk of the ship's forward armor. The second alien ship fared much the same. The shields of the third collapsed much sooner, though. Three of the missiles from Defense Platform Alpha smashed into its hull, their detonations tearing away most of its forward armor and even managing to piece its forward structure. The third alien ship was also knocked slightly off course by the explosion of the final missile. It righted itself quickly to rejoin the others.

The *Pinket*'s captain was screaming over the comm. for assistance. Marcus could see the *Pinket*'s shield was failing, and as good as her helmsman was, no one could dodge the near constant streams of fire that the alien destroyers continued to spit towards her.

The other defense platforms around Cerebus VI who were in a position to fire on the approaching alien destroyers joined the fight. Volley after volley of missiles went hurling through the void towards the alien destroyers. They weren't able to save the *Pinket*. Whether they felt threatened by the inbound mass of missiles from the defense platforms around the planet, or they had just grown tired of the game they had been playing with her, two of the alien destroyers increased their speed. They overtook the *Pinket*, flanking her. Energy blasts speared both of her sides, burning away what remained of her shields and slicing through her armor. The *Pinket* died in a flash of white light so bright that Mikal had to look away from Defense Platform Alpha's main screen.

"Frag it to Hades," Commander Threshal yelled.

Marcus felt her pain. All those men and woman aboard the *Hagel* and the *Pinket* had died for nothing. Neither ship had been able to fire so much as a single shot at the alien destroyers. Marcus did find some solace though as the volleys of missiles from the platforms reached the alien vessels. The destroyers didn't appear to have any ECMs. If so, they surely would have used them. Close-in defensive guns opened up on the missiles, thinning out their numbers, but it wasn't enough to stop them all.

The lead alien destroyer was completely overwhelmed. It exploded as missile after missile rammed into it. The second of the alien destroyers broke hard to port, veering upwards, in an effort to avoid the bulk of the missiles closing on it. Solar Federation missiles weren't simply mindless ballistics, though.

They changed course as well, plowing into the alien destroyer's weaker, underside armor. It reeled sideways, leaking atmosphere in the wake of the missile's attack. It was impossible to tell if the destroyer was truly dead in space or merely stunned into a momentary drift as its crew fought to return it to action. The third destroyer, already damaged, died as violently as the first had.

Mikal let out of whoop of triumph as the alien ships died. Marcus might have joined him except that he had been watching actions of the large alien vessel he could only think of as a super dreadnought, as it laid waste to the shipyards scattered about the Cerebus system. Commander Threshal had been right in stating that the Endeavor's fighters wouldn't be enough. The Endeavor's fighters had done their best, many pilots even making the ultimate sacrifice by ramming their own ship into an alien missile after they expended their onboard munitions. Even so, the Endeavor lost her shields to the vast amount of missiles that still struck her. The alien super dreadnought wasted no time in finishing her. A beam of energy, as wide as the *Hagel* had been, lashed out from it and cut the shipyard in half along its length like a scalpel. The Endeavor broke apart, crumbling to bits of charred metal, as small explosions began to erupt all throughout her remains. With her died all the ships under construction in her extended work branches. The alien super dreadnought didn't stop with the Endeavor. She had been only the beginning. It systematically targeted the other shipyards as well, one after another, until they were all nothing more than charred and drifting debris.

As the last shipyard perished, the fleet of alien destroyers who had been holding back around the edges of the jump point all sprang forward together. Their engines blazed hot as they raced towards Cerebus VI.

Marcus knew Orbital Defense Platform Alpha and all the others like her would be dead in moments even as Commander Threshal started barking orders.

"Target them all!" she roared. "Fire at will! Fire at will!"

****

Admiral Perron blinked in surprise and read the report again. The words on the screen in front of him refused to change as he read them the second time. Wide-eyed and in disbelief, he looked up at Captain Jerry Malcom who stood in front of his desk.

"We've lost the Cerebus VI system?" Admiral Perron asked.

"It would appear so, sir," Captain Malcom nodded.

"To who?" Perron demanded.

"At this time, we're still trying to determine that, sir," Malcom said. "What little data we received from the drones that were dispatched into the system, before they were destroyed, point to a massive fleet of alien hostiles. Their origins and motivations are completely unknown, sir. I can tell you, however, that they have at least two super dreadnaughts and over five dozen lesser warships in the system. The drones also detected large amounts of jump point activity, so that number could be continuing to grow even as we speak."

"I see." Admiral Perron cracked his knuckles, scowling at Captain Malcom.

"Earth Gov. is in an uproar, sir," Malcom said. "The counsel is demanding that we take action at once as there are over three hundred million civilians on Cerebus VI."

"And the Cerebus shipyards?" Perron asked.

"Lost, sir," Captain Malcom told him. "All of them."

"I hate Mondays," Perron muttered, rubbing at his temples and trying to reduce the increasing level of stress that grew inside him.

"Sir, it's Thursday," Captain Malcom corrected him politely.

"Is it now?" Perron shrugged. "Feels like a Monday to me."

Captain Malcom handed him a tablet. "These are the battlegroups we have within quick striking distance of the Cerebus system, sir. None of them alone have the number of ships or firepower to go head to head alone against the alien vessels already in the system, though."

Perron took the tablet and began scanning over the list on its screen.

"The longer we wait, sir..." Captain Malcom started but fell quiet as soon as Perron's glaring eyes rose to meet his own.

"I am aware of the dangers of hesitation on our part, Captain," Perron said, trying to keep his tone calm and professional. "You have family on Cerebus VI, don't you, Captain?"

"Yes, sir," Captain Malcom said, nodding. "My sister moved to the planet two years ago."

"My condolences, Captain, but we can't allow personal matters to cloud our judgement. If we just send ships into the Cerebus system, guns blazing and without a proper plan or better still, more intel on what we are facing there, those ships will die just like those who were in the Cerebus system did when the aliens arrived."

"I understand that, sir," Captain Malcom said, standing perhaps a touch straighter as he answered.

"Right now, these aliens hold the advantage. They outnumber any force we have on hand to throw at them, and they may know a good deal more about us and what we are and our tech than we know about them. And that's not even considering Cerebus VI. If they didn't just slag the planet from space, those three hundred million souls you mentioned may very well be hostages."

"Still, Admiral," Captain Malcom pleaded. "We have to do something."

"We are," Perron assured him. "Leave me. I'll have your orders to you within the hour."

"Yes, sir." Captain Malcom gave him a sharp nod and whirled about on his heels, leaving Perron's office.

Admiral Perron sighed and began to study the list of available battlegroups and ships much more intensely. He had to weigh his options very carefully, because the fate of every soul still alive in the Cerebus system was going to hinge on what he decided.

****

Captain Shannon Weber sat atop a container of small arms munitions staring out at the stars inside one of the *Thrawn*'s lower level storage bays. It was a spot he often came to when he needed time to think or smoke. He might be the *Thrawn*'s captain, but regulations were regulations, and it was his job to set an example for his crew. He couldn't be caught chain-smoking his way through an entire pack of black market cigarettes. Shannon had made a promise to himself that he would quit smoking with each promotion he had gotten over the last four years of his service, from when he started in the Solar Federations' army as an infantryman to his transfer into the Navy. His survival of each bloodbath his career and bad luck had flung him into had only increased his rank but had done nothing to relieve his dependence on nicotine. His fingertips were blunted and his teeth were stained a nasty shade of yellow, but those who knew him or served under him knew all too well to bring those things up to his face. Shannon was too smart to truly believe his crew and superiors thought he had quit, but he kept up the pretense of having done so because bringing the whole mess out into the open would only cause bigger problems than having to find a solitary and secluded spot to indulge in his nasty habit.

He had received word of the fate of the Cerebus system an hour before. That kind of news got to anyone who had a trace of humanity within them. With all the up close and personal death he had seen in his career, it was tough to believe that he could feel anything at all, but he did. The news combined with the orders that came along with it had driven him down here to smoke. Shannon firmly believed that the nicotine coursing through his body helped him to focus and think clearer. If he had ever needed a smoke to get himself together, it was today. The reports on the strength of the alien ships in system at Cerebus were beyond worrisome. He didn't doubt for a second that they had transports of some kind among their numbers or that their troops had made planet-fall. Alien or not, the only reason for them to enter the Cerebus system in such numbers and such a hostile fashion was because there was something on Cerebus VI that they wanted and wanted bad. Nothing else made sense. That's where he and his men came in.

His ship, the *Thrawn*, wasn't a normal ship of the line. She was one of two battleship/transport hybrids that the Solar Federation had in its fleet. The *Thrawn* could trade blows with the best battleships that Solar Federation had at her disposal, and on a good day, maybe even go head to head to with a super dreadnought and survive long enough to escape in one piece. She had some serious teeth. She also had her own fighter squadrons, small ones sure by real Navy standards, but two of them. They added to the defense capabilities of her top of the line Electronic Countermeasure and point defense weapons. Her shields were twice as strong as a normal ship her size and her engines equally as powerful. And the *Thrawn* was far from being a small ship. She was half the size of a super dreadnought, though most of the space was given over to her engines and bays. What made her special though, in truth, was that she carried a full division of elite, special ops. shock troopers with the tanks and APCs to support them. When you needed to get in, drop troops, kick the crap of someone, and get out alive, the *Thrawn* was the ship you sent in to do it. Her sister ship, the *Galaxicon,* was newer, yes, perhaps a hair better in design, but Shannon and his men on the *Thrawn* were veterans. The *Thrawn* had seen a lot of action both during the Solar Federation's last civil war, which had last only a matter of brutal, hard fought weeks, and on the frontier. As luck would have it, the *Thrawn* was also closer to the Cerebus system at present time. Shannon could understand why Admiral Perron had chosen him for the mission he had been given, but that didn't mean he had to be happy about it or even like it. Decking Perron might be a court-martial offense, but it would sure make Shannon feel good.

His orders were for the *Thrawn* to accompany the taskforce being dispatched into the Cerebus system, assist them in the space battle if possible while in route to Cerebus VI, and then retake the planet from whatever alien forces that might be occupying it. As tough as his ship and his men were, Shannon knew their odds of making it out of this were pretty slim as all data pointed to the aliens having a vast superiority in numbers and perhaps tech that the Solar Federation's best and brightest may not have even began to dream of yet. Shannon hated unknowns. They got folks killed. And this whole mess was full of them.

Shannon took a last drag from his cigarette before grinding it out on the top of the container he was sitting on. He flicked the butt into the pile of them lying against the bottom of the bay wall next to him and hopped down from the container. He didn't like any of what lay ahead of him, but orders were orders, and he had a job to do.

On his way to the *Thrawn*'s bridge, his XO, Williams, met up with him. Williams smirked at him, waving a hand in the air in front of his nose as if he were fanning away a bad odor.

"I see you were able to squeeze in a moment to find some peace, sir," Williams said.

Shannon didn't bother to answer Williams with words, he just growled at the man.

Williams went pale. "Sorry, sir. I guess I forget myself for a second there."

"There are a lot of things I will put up with on this ship, Williams, but that isn't one of them. Do I make myself clear?" Shannon asked, scowling as he did so.

Williams nodded, his head bobbing up and down in rapid motion.

"If you weren't new to this ship, we'd be having this conversation after you woke up in medical," Shannon said in a dead serious tone.

"Won't happen again, sir," Williams croaked.

The two of them reached the lift at the end of the corridor they had been walking down. Its doors swished open to admit them.

"Bridge," Shannon told the lift's AI.

Shannon turned to Williams. "I've seen your file. I know you've been through a lot and can take some heavy crap. You need to know though that aboard this ship, we don't always play things by the book. The crewmembers of the *Thrawn*, statistically speaking, have the shortest life expectancies of any in the entire Solar Federation fleet and with good reason. When the crap hits the fan, we're the ones who deal with it and clean it up. You will show everyone aboard this ship the proper respect, Williams, or you'll find yourself transferred off her or dead so fast you won't even know happened."

"I'll keep that in mind," Williams answered.

"See that you do," Shannon said as the lift doors opened again and the two of them stepped onto the bridge.

Shannon headed straight for his command chair and plopped into it. There was no call of "captain on deck" as there might have been aboard most other ships of the fleet. His presence was simply noted as the bridge crew continued on with their work.

Williams moved to stand beside Shannon's chair. "Helmsman, estimated time until we rendezvous with Taskforce Hammer?"

"My name is Redder, sir," the helmsman answered him.

Williams glanced at Shannon who appeared to be stifling a laugh.

"Redder then," Williams corrected himself.

"We should be dropping out of jump space in less than two minutes, sir," Redder answered.

Shannon had to admit to himself he was enjoying watching his new XO squirm. Williams, as uptight and by the book as he was, likely thought he had just been assigned to a command in Hell. Shannon had made a habit of addressing his crew by name. It made each of them feel more important as he saw things and helped morale, but he also made sure they knew who was in command. He had a rep of coming down hard on anyone who showed disrespect or got out of line, and he liked it that way. Respect was good, but so was fear, and he liked to have both.

"Not sure we can really call Hammer a real Taskforce," Shannon commented.

Williams shrugged. "It's everything the Federation could scrap together on such short notice."

"Exactly," Shannon laughed. "One super dreadnought, seven battleships, and their screening destroyers. That's not much given what we do know about what's waiting for us in the Cerebus system."

"Admiral Early is command of Hammer," Williams pointed out. "I've met her. She really is the best of the best."

"I've met her, too." Shannon's mood turned dark, but he didn't say anything more.

"Then you know how good she is?" Williams asked.

Shannon changed the subject. "I imagine Admiral Early will want to come aboard for a meeting before we make the second jump to Cerebus. Make sure things are ready for her and the other captains, Williams."

"Yes, sir," the new XO nodded and left the bridge.

****

The *Thrawn* shot through the open jump point into the Cassallia system. The ships of Taskforce Hammer were there waiting on her. Redder slowed the *Thrawn* and brought her into the taskforce's formation. She was the second largest ship present. Only Admiral Early's flagship, the super dreadnought, *Castle*, was larger.

Just as Captain Weber had predicted, one of Admiral Early's aides hailed the *Thrawn* informing Williams that the admiral, accompanied by the other ranking captains of the taskforce, would be coming aboard at oh three hundred hours. Williams had met the admiral before, but given his almost hero worship of her command skills, he was nervous about doing so again.

Shuttles began carrying over the ranking captains of the taskforce a solid half hour before the meeting was to take place. Williams, accompanied by two of Weber's grunts acting as honor guards, met each in turn. He escorted them to the *Thrawn*'s war room. Hastily prepared refreshments consisting of iced water, coffee, wine, and a varied assortment of biscuits were arranged on a small display next to room's conference table. Williams made sure each of the captains were comfortable before scurrying away to greet the next one coming aboard.

After all four of the taskforce's senior captains were aboard, Admiral Early arrived. Williams watched the docking doors of her shuttle slid open as his heart fluttered in his chest. Two armored and heavily armed troopers marched off the shuttle, the metal bottoms of their boots clanging against the corridor floor with each step they took. They assumed positions beside the shuttle's door, their rifles displayed in their arms. Only then did Admiral Early emerge from the shuttle. Williams' breath caught at the sight of her. Her dress uniform did its best to mask the curves of her well-toned and youthful body, but it simply couldn't hide the fact that she was one hundred percent woman and a very beautiful one at that. Samantha Early was the youngest person in the history of the Solar Federation Navy to hold the rank of admiral. She had been top of her class at the academy and then went on to win victory after victory, usually against overwhelming odds. It didn't hurt that her brother also sat on the Solar Federation counsel. Rumors claimed that the two of them weren't close, but in politics, sometimes it was only one's family name that mattered.

Admiral Samantha Early's skin was pale. Williams knew she seldom took shore leave or visited her home on Earth. Her career was her life. She appeared to thrive when pushed to her limits, and there was no better place for that than the Solar Federation's frontier regions where she held power as the ranking fleet office.

Williams imagined that senior Admiral Perron had called in a good deal of favors to get the counsel to concede to risk one of the Navy's finest officers on such a dire and dangerous mission as the one Taskforce Hammer had been assigned. However, Admiral Early was the perfect for the job. If anyone could deal with all the unknowns and overwhelming numbers that the taskforce faced, it was her.

Williams found himself staring at the admiral longer than he should. Her red hair, pulled tight behind her head, was as fierce and hypnotic as her cold, green eyes. Tearing his eyes away, he glanced at the two of Weber's grunts flanking him. Both of them looked out of place compared to the guards that had accompanied Admiral Early. Their armor was carbon-scarred, and judging by their unkempt appearances, it was a blessing that they didn't reek of body odor or something worse. If the Admiral minded, she hid it well.

"It's my sincere pleasure to welcome you—" Williams started, but Admiral Early interrupted him.

"Where is Captain Weber?" she demanded.

"I can only assume that the captain is awaiting you with the other officers in the war room ma'am. Was there something you needed to see him about before we proceed there?"

Admiral Early's laugh was loud and full. "For such a suicidal manic on the battlefield, Shannon can be rather the coward at times."

Williams didn't reply. He had no idea what she was talking about. Instead, he just put on his best smile and waited to see what Admiral Early did next.

As if seeing him truly for the first time, her laughter ceased and her demeanor became professional again. "We've met, haven't we?" she asked, extending her hand to him. Williams took it, returning her friendly shake.

"We have," he said beaming, delighted that she remembered. "I am currently serving as Captain Weber's XO."

"Right then." Admiral Early withdrew her hand from his politely. "It's Williams, isn't it?"

"Yes, ma'am, it is." His smile grew broader across his lips. "If you will follow me, I will take you to Captain Weber and the others."

Admiral Early nodded and followed Williams towards the nearby lift.

Her personal guards remained at the doorway of her shuttle.

When they reached the war room, the other captains had all taken seats around the room's large table. Some of them were sipping on wine, one of them on coffee. Captain Weber sat at the lower end of the table opposite from Admiral Early would be sitting.

Williams noticed that she gave Captain Weber a smirking glance as she entered and took her seat.

"I'm sure you all know why we're here," Admiral Early began. "The Cerebus system has been overrun and occupied by an alien force whose sheer numbers alone are enough to give anyone in their right mind pause in challenging them. We have no idea what technological advances these aliens may possess, but it's up to us to kick their butts and send them running back to wherever they came from."

Early snapped her fingers at Williams and gestured from him to bring her a glass of ice water. Williams hurried to do so as she continued.

"We need a plan on how we're going to make the most of what we have available to us. Under other circumstances, the ships of Taskforce Hammer would be considered a sizable fleet. Against these alien intruders, though, we can expect to be outnumbered at least four to one, with their numbers continuing to increase, based on the intel the last wave of drones launched into the Cerebus system sent back."

Captain Martin raised his hand like a child at school. Early nodded, acknowledging him.

"How did these aliens get so many ships into the system so quickly?" Captain Martin asked.

"Short answer is that we don't really know. Long answer is that their jump tech appears to be well ahead of our own. They are able to open jump points beyond the like of which we have ever seen and worse, sustain them for what appears to be indefinite periods of time," Admiral Early answered. "The two, massive, lead warships that we've classified as super dreadnoughts are one point five times as large my own flagship, the *Castle*. By the time Taskforce Hammer arrives in the Cerebus system, it is entirely possible that three, perhaps even four, of these super dreadnoughts will have joined the enemy's numbers there."

The gathered senior captains muttered darkly among themselves as Admiral Early paused to accept the water Williams brought her and took a slug of it before placing it in front of her on the table. Captain Weber didn't join in their side conversations. His eyes and attention remained glued to Admiral Early.

"I've seen the same data you have, Admiral," Weber spoke up. "It's true their warp tech seems superior to our own, but from what I gather, their shield tech is inferior. Numbers don't mean crap if you can reduce them before they matter."

"Agreed," Admiral Early frowned, "but we also know their weapons are on par with our own, perhaps better even at close range."

"So we hit them hard, hit them fast, and don't let them get into beam weapon range," Captain Weber suggested. "We've been in spots as bad as this one before and came through just fine."

Williams caught that there was a hidden reference in Captain Weber's words. Shannon had never fully answered him in regards to how well he knew Admiral Early. Williams was beginning to suspect that the two of them knew each other very well indeed. The interplay between the two of them seemed to indicate a relationship far closer and deeper than a merely professional one. The thought of it made his stomach turn. Early was everything a fleet officer aspired to be while Weber was the epitome of a loose cannon and a slightly mad one at that given how he ran the *Thrawn* so informally.

"If Captain Weber is correct," Captain Hudson jumped in, "then maybe we should just go in guns blazing. We'll have the advantage of surprise on our side. By catching them off guard in such a manner, perhaps we can reduce their numbers before the aliens are able to bring them bear on us."

Admiral Early shook her head. "This is a military operation, gentlemen, not a game of king of the hill. We need to be sure we are in a position that will not only give us the initial advantage you're talking about but a sustained one as well. The last thing we want is to get caught in a straight up line-to-line crossfire against the kind of numbers these aliens have."

"If you'll all take a gander at the battle plan I've just sent to your respective screens," Captain Weber addressed those gathered around the table, "I think you'll like what you see."

Admiral Early scowled at Weber, looking to Williams as if she wanted to tear his head from his shoulders and fling it across the war room, before she checked her own screen to examine the plan he had come up with on the fly.

"Not bad," she said after a few moments. "I think with a little fiddling, we can make this work."

The admission sounded as if it was a hard one for her to make, but Williams knew that Early was a professional to the core. If another officer came up with something that worked, she wasn't the sort of leader who overruled them to implement her own plan just because she should. There was, however, a twinkle in her eyes as she added, "I like that the *Thrawn* will be taking the brunt of enemy fire as we jump in…" her expression softened, "but can we afford to take the risk of her being too heavily damaged to complete her own mission?"

"The *Thrawn* is one of the toughest ships around, ma'am." Captain Weber made his last word sound almost like an insult instead of a term of respect. "She can take it. Besides, my ship was never intended to do anything more than reach Cerebus VI and land there. It's my job to handle things planet-side while you deal with hostiles in the stars. If you screw up, we likely won't be leaving anyway."

Admiral Early smiled. "Good point. So the *Thrawn* and the taskforce's destroyers will come in hot, jumping into a position that allows them to engage the bulk of the enemy's battleships. The *Thrawn* will then proceed to make a run for the planet while the destroyers continue to draw the enemy's attention. The *Castle* and the taskforce's battleships will jump in as close as possible to the enemy's super dreadnoughts, and Lord willing, pound them to dust before they are to fully react to our presence. All ships of Taskforce Hammer will then regroup and withdraw in system, drawing the attention of the enemy fleet in pursuit, while the *Thrawn*'s ground forces do what they can to re-secure Cerebus VI and save those that they can there."

"I like this plan." Captain Martin grinned, showing his too-white teeth. Martin was the best-dressed captain at the meeting and Williams could see that the man had a flare for promptness and fashion.

"If we're all in agreement then, we'll implement this plan at oh eight hundred hours. That should give us all a few hours to get our ships and crews prepared as well as with a bit of luck catch some rest before we go jumping into Hell."

No one disagreed. The meeting finished up. It was followed by various private conversations among the captains as they stuck around chatting as if at a social gathering before they began to drift out of the war room one by one.

Through it all, Captain Weber kept his seat. He didn't get up from it until only he and the admiral remained with Williams watching them.

"You took that pretty well," Captain Weber laughed, referring to his out of the blue battle plan.

"I suppose I should expect crap like that out of you by now." Admiral Early smiled.

"Yeah, you probably should," Weber agreed.

"It's been quite some time," Early said, changing the subject.

"Too long or not long enough?" Weber quipped.

"Ask me when all this is over," Early told him and then turned her back on Weber, heading for the war room's door.

Williams was utterly stunned by the exchange. He was frozen in place, apparently for too long. Shannon Weber walked over and gave him a nudge, whispering, "You better get to it and see her back to her shuttle, Williams. Admirals don't walk alone, ya know?"

"Yes, sir!" Williams blurted out and raced to catch up to Admiral Early.

****

After escorting Admiral Early back to her shuttle and seeing her off safely on her return trip to the *Castle*, Williams headed for the *Thrawn*'s bridge. Captain Weber was already there when he arrived and preparations for the jump into the Cerebus system were underway. Normally, it would have been his job as XO to oversee such undertakings, but aboard the *Thrawn*, apparently he wasn't needed. Despite the slacker appearance of her crew and the informal attitude of her captain, they were not the screw-ups they seemed to be. In fact, Williams had never seen such a fine-tuned crew as the *Thrawn*'s was right now.

Weber must have noticed his expression because he called out, "Don't worry, newbie. You'll get used to it."

"Captain Weber, I must say…"

Weber stopped him right there. "Shannon," Weber gently reminded him. "Unless use of rank is needed, you will address me as Shannon or if must be, *sir*."

"Sir," Williams said after taking a moment to compose himself, "what are my orders?"

"Sit back and enjoy the show until you're needed." Shannon Weber grinned at him.

"And when will that be?" Williams asked.

"The second we jump into Cerebus." Shannon's grin fell from his face. "Just trust your instincts. I know you have them. You'll see when you need to hop in and when to keep out of the way of my crew and let them do their jobs. Trust me."

Williams nodded, feigning a polite smile, as inwardly he realized just how screwed in the head a captain like Weber had to be. Maybe it was from his time in the infantry and Special Forces before transferring into the Navy or maybe it was just who Shannon was. Either way, the man was a certifiable lunatic in Williams' opinion.

"Take the chair," Shannon ordered him. "I'm going to grab some rest before the shooting starts up. Wake me at oh five hundred if I'm not already back. You have the conn."

"Yes, sir." Williams accepted command. He watched Shannon leave the bridge as he eased into the command chair Shannon had vacated.

As soon as Shannon was gone, the helmsman, Redder, turned to him. "So how did it go?"

"How did what go, crewman?" Williams asked, surprised by the question and unsure what Redder was asking about.

"The old man and the admiral coming face to face again?" Redder said as if Williams should know exactly what he was talking about.

It took Williams a fraction of a second to put together that "the old man" was a term of respect for Captain Weber.

"The meeting went fine, I suppose," Williams answered. "Should it have gone otherwise?"

Most of the bridge crew broke into laughter.

"You're really clueless, aren't you?" Redder chuckled and then hastily added the word "Sir" as he appeared to remember who he was talking to.

"Apparently, I am, Mr. Redder," Williams confessed. "Would you be so kind as to fill me in on what it is that I missing?"

"The old man and the admiral," Redder said carefully, "They used to..." Redder paused as if searching for the proper word.

"The two of them used to have a *thing,* sir," Krystal, the communications officer, chimed in, saving Redder from likely making an idiot out of himself.

"Indeed?" Williams asked, not wanting to believe what he was hearing, though it made sense given how the Admiral and Captain Weber had behaved around one another.

"I ain't messing with you, sir," Redder swore. "A few years back, the two of them were all hot and heavy."

"And this relationship ended on bad terms, I take it?" Williams asked.

"That might be the understatement of the eon," Krystal sighed.

"Rumors say they got into it so badly they almost killed each other. The old man supposedly almost got kicked out of the fleet for it. The admiral wasn't an admiral back then, but she was still the fleet's golden child, up-and-coming hotshot. All she got from what I heard was a slap on the wrist," Redder explained.

Williams cleared his throat. "I fail to see how all this is any of my business or yours, Mr. Redder. Do you not have a jump point to calculate?"

"Yes, sir," Redder nodded.

"Then I suggest you get to work on doing so. Now," Williams ordered.

Silence fell over the bridge as everyone returned to their work, and Williams sat staring at the stars on the forward view screen.

****

Shannon caught a couple of hours sleep and a quick smoke before returning to the bridge earlier than planned. He sipped on black coffee as he watched the timer tick down to the moment of the *Thrawn*'s jump into Cerebus. Seeing Samantha again had gone much better than it could have. He noticed she had come aboard with a sidearm on her hip. Whether it had been for him or merely part of the formal dress uniform protocol that he had managed to avoid was a good question. If anything, her treatment of him during the meeting and afterwards was more than just her normally cold, professional demeanor. At times during their encounter, he had almost allowed himself to believe there were still feelings between that weren't bloodlust and anger. Shannon didn't suppose it mattered, though. The past was the past, and sometimes it was best to leave it there.

He could feel the subtle vibrations in the floor of the bridge that meant the ship's engines were spinning up for the jump into Cerebus. Shannon glanced at Williams. The XO was faring much better than he had expected. He didn't doubt that Williams would live up to his file when the crap hit the fan.

"All systems green. We are cleared for jump," Redder announced.

Shannon met the helmsman's eyes and nodded at him.

"And...jumping now," Redder exclaimed.

The atmosphere of the bridge grew a touch colder, making Shannon shiver, as space folded around the hull of the *Thrawn* and she jumped into the Cerebus system. All twelve of Taskforce Hammer's destroyers jumped with her.

The stars on the bridge's main view screen blinked out of existence as a new set of stars took their place. Then, all Hell broke loose as Shannon screamed, "All batteries, fire at will!"

The *Thrawn* found herself facing a virtual wall of enemy battleships. The aliens were just as taken by surprise as Shannon had hoped they would be. They sat motionless among the stars as the *Thrawn's* weapons blazed and tore into their ranks. Missiles left her tubes in volley after volley, streaking towards their targets even as her forward railguns ripped away at the shields and armor of the closest enemy battleships. The destroyers of Taskforce Hammer that had made the jump with the *Thrawn* added their firepower to her own. Two of the alien battleships died in flames before they could even respond to the threat which had appeared out of nowhere.

Shannon had never seen ships like the alien vessels. They were rough-looking, overly armored monstrosities with none of the stylized sleekness of Solar Federation ships. Despite their awkward and primitive appearance though, they were fast and their crews had to be well trained. The trio of battleships that the *Thrawn* had shifted her fire onto after eliminating her first two targets initiated evasive maneuvers that set them rolling in space. Two veered upwards, over the *Thrawn*, while the third one dove below her. The tactic would have been a brilliant one if Shannon had planned on keeping the *Thrawn* where she was. He had no intention of doing so, however. The idea was to plow through the alien ships and push beyond them.

The alien battleships and the Federation destroyers that had accompanied the *Thrawn* continued to trade blows. The destroyers were smaller the battleships, but their usual advantages in speed and maneuverability were nullified by the alien battleships' own speed. They weaved about in space, matching every move of the Federation destroyers.

Shannon saw that the *Thrawn* wasn't going to have any problem punching through their ranks. His accompanying destroyers, however, were going to be locked into an engagement they couldn't possibly hope to win. That left him with two choices: stick to the plan and leave the destroyers to die or hang back with them to lend them what aid he could. It really wasn't much of a choice.

"Slow us down!" Shannon shouted at Redder. "Redirect all fire towards the battleships we just tore through."

"Sir," Williams said. "That isn't our mission, sir!"

"I'm well aware of that, Williams," Shannon told his XO. "Taskforce Hammer needs every ship it has, though. If we can save a few of those destroyers out there…"

"Enemy battleships are powering up close-range weapons!" Shannon's Tactical Officer Rubble warned.

So far, the *Thrawn's* advanced Electronic Countermeasures and shields had kept the battle-carrier largely unscathed. That wasn't going to last though, and Shannon knew it.

The missiles from the *Thrawn's* aft launchers had found their targets. One alien battleship skewed sideways as its shields collapsed and explosions flashed along its portside hull. Another's shields glowed bright blue as missiles hammered it in a series of volleys designed to overwhelm those shields and take them down.

The *Thrawn* shook as energy beams from two nearby alien destroyers met and concentrated themselves on the battle-carrier's stern.

"Shields at sixty-three percent and dropping," Rubble called out.

"Return fire!" Shannon ordered. "Target their weapon arrays!"

It had become clear to Shannon that the spikes randomly spaced over the hulls of the alien battleships were the conductors for their beam weapons. Energy would dance up and between them, coalescing there before being spat towards its intended target. As thus, if those spikes were taken out, so were the battleship's close in energy weapons.

Shannon watched as the *Thrawn*'s railguns raked over the hull of one of the alien battleships. They laid waste to the spikes covering its hull. One set of spikes were in the process of powering up as the railgun fire swept over them. The ensuring explosion blew the alien battleship apart in a flash of light and heat. He allowed himself a grin as the alien battleship died.

Of the twelve destroyers that had made the jump into the Cerebus system alongside the *Thrawn*, only six remained. Thanks to Shannon offering up the *Thrawn* as a target by slowing to prolong her engagement with the formation of alien battleships, those destroyers had been able to break away from the battle. They were high-tailing it to join up with the rest of Taskforce

Hammer. There was nothing more Shannon could do for them now. He had to focus on getting the *Thrawn* out of the swarm of alien battleships surrounding her before they could concentrate their fire and do more damage than they already had.

"Adjust course for Cerebus VI, engines at full," Shannon ordered. "Light 'em up as we go!"

The advantage of surprise was gone, but the *Thrawn* was an extremely powerful and large ship. Her heavy, forward railguns punched a hole through the formation of alien battleships that were trying desperately to block her path and trap her amongst their numbers. Pieces of debris from the shattered and broken hulls of alien battleships careened through the void as the *Thrawn* drove on straight through them.

Only when the *Thrawn* was clear of the formation of alien battleships did Shannon turn his attention to finding out how the rest of Taskforce Hammer had fared as it entered the Cerebus system.

****

Admiral Early stood on the bridge of the Solar Federation superdreadnought, the *Castle*, as it plunged through the jump point it had created into the Cerebus system. The seven battleships attached to it had actually made the jump first. They were already dropping like falling icicles towards the alien super dreadnought that had parked itself in the center of the system.

The *Ironside* and the *Stark* opened fire with their forward beam weapons while the *Graf, Stockholm, Europa, Kirk,* and *Dagger* emptied their ready missile tubes at the monstrous ship they approached. The combined fire of all the battleships struck the alien super dreadnought's shields like a hammer. The alien super dreadnought's shields glowed like a wall of blue fire under their assault.

The aliens' own battleships were spread out through the system. They weren't clustered about the two super dreadnoughts as Early had feared they might be. And the second alien super dreadnought was far, far out of range of this engagement, thank God. It appeared to be in orbit around Cerebus VI. That might cause problems for Shannon and the *Thrawn*, but it was a very good thing for own attack group.

"All weapons target that monster and fire at will!" Early ordered.

The *Castle* was a massive ship in its own right, but even so, the alien super dreadnought was one point five times its size. It looked tough enough to eat entire planets for breakfast, and as it began to return fire on her battleships, Early almost believed that it could. Even as the *Castle's* primary beam weapons blazed away at its shields, the alien super dreadnought vomited a deluge of missiles that flooded the space between the two giant ships. The CO of the alien super dreadnought had made the same call

Early would have made herself if she had been in the alien CO's position, opting to ignore the battleships and go after the real threat, which in this case, was her ship, the *Castle*.

There was no such thing as evasive maneuvers for super dreadnought class ships at the range at which the *Castle* and the alien monster were engaged at. All Early could do was brace for the monster's fire and hope the *Castle's* shields could handle it. The *Castle's* Electronic Countermeasures played havoc with the inbound missiles. Many of them veered off course, losing their target completely. Some even turned, head on, into the sides of the missiles next to them as the darkness of space was lit up by detonating warheads. The crews of the *Castle's* close in, point defense weapons as well her automated ones, raked the ranks of the missiles with heavy railgun fire. Streams of rounds slashed at the missiles, knocking some off course, leaving others bleeding fuel and dead in space, and blowing others to shreds. If the data was correct, the *Castle's* defenses stopped a staggering three hundred missiles from making contact. As an impressive of a feat as that was, it still wasn't enough to leave the *Castle* unscathed. Somewhere around one hundred missiles had managed to get through all of her defenses. They slammed against her shields in flashes of white and yellow.

Admiral Early flinched as the bridge's forward screen went white from the blasts of the enemy missiles striking the *Castle's* shields. She had to turn her eyes away the light was so intense. Her knees almost gave way beneath her, but she knew that was her mind was playing tricks on her and not the *Castle* actually being jarred about by the attack. The *Castle* was too massive for even an attack such as this one to shake her to her core.

"Forward shields taking heavy fire!" her tactical officer said, reporting the obvious.

"Damage?" Early snapped at him.

"Shields at thirty-three percent and holding!" the officer yelled back at her.

"Increase power to forward shields!" Early's XO ordered.

"Belay that!" Early overrode him. "Hold our course and increase power to the forward energy weapons arrays!"

"Ma'am!" Her XO blurted at her, but a glare from her that threatened murder shut him up.

Early was playing chicken with an alien monster of a vessel of that was larger than even her own super dreadnought, but this was the kind of crap she lived for, and she was dang good at it.

The seven battleships had by now long passed the alien super dreadnought and altered their course to intercept the surviving Federation destroyers from the group that had accompanied the *Thrawn* into the Cerebus system. They should be well clear of the blast if this works, she thought.

The *Castle*'s forward energy weapons fired again. This time, their beams were thicker and burned brighter as they touched the alien super dreadnought's shields. Those shields strained to absorb the fury raining onto them and failed. Early watched them flicker and then fade. The *Castle* kept up its relentless attack, though. Her beams reached the hull of the alien super dreadnought. Armor bubbled and foamed at the points where they touched it. Then they were cutting into the alien super dreadnought's body. Atmosphere sprayed from the holes the beams dug, spraying into the void like eruptions of hissing steam.

Admiral Early held her breath as she waited for fate to deal her hand as her helmsman screamed, "Contact in fifteen seconds!"

"Admiral!" her XO yelled again, almost begging with the tone of his voice.

Her XO might not realize it or perhaps just don't want to accept the truth, but it was already too late for the *Castle* to turn away. One way or another, the Federation super dreadnought was going *through* the alien monster whose image filled her forward view screen.

The *Castle*'s beam weapons continued to burn into the alien super dreadnought. Explosion rippled across its entire body now and not just at the points where the *Castle*'s weapons were cutting it. Blasts of fire jutted outwards from the sides of its hull like volcanoes hurling molten magma into space.

"Eight seconds!" her helmsman shrieked, his eyes wide and glued to the station in front of him.

Sweat beaded on Admiral Early's brow. A drop of it ran into her right eye. She blinked it away, batting her long eyelashes. "Hold course!" she ordered a final time.

With three seconds to spare before the *Castle* made contact with the alien super dreadnought, the monstrous ship blew apart.

"Brace for impact!" Early howled, diving for her command chair. She managed to make it into the chair and hold on for dear life as the *Castle* punched through the spinning debris and heat of the exploding alien super dreadnought.

This time, the *Castle* did rock. The Federation super dreadnought shook, and the deck of the bridge vibrated as if the massive ship was attempting to enter the atmosphere of a planet. Her shields spiked in a flash of blue and died before failing completely. She held together, though. The *Castle* emerged from the wreckage of the exploding alien super dreadnought, a fireball in her own right. Most of the fire though wasn't from her. It died out quickly on her hull, extinguished by her speed and the cold void of space.

Cheers and cries of victory rang out all over the bridge around Admiral Early as she righted herself in her command chair. She had only barely managed to keep herself from being flung out it and sent toppling towards the forward view screen. The death grip she had clutched the arms of her chair with had cost her two nails that been torn away from the flesh they had been attached too. It hurt like Hell, but she didn't care. Her crew was alive. She was alive. And the alien bastards were dead.

Ignoring the pain, she gritted her teeth and went back to work. The alien super dreadnought might be dead, but the battle was by no means over. Scores of alien battleships and destroyers were now pushing their engines to the max to reach the *Castle*. While most of the enemy battleships were well out of range and in pursuit of Shannon aboard the *Thrawn*, not all of them were. Those that weren't joined the enemy destroyers in their attempt to close in on and engage the *Castle*. Some of them had launched volleys of missiles despite their range. Early wasn't too worried about those missiles yet, though. She had managed to stab at the screen on the arm of her command chair with one of her uninjured fingers and call up a data burst that allowed her a fast glance at what damage the *Castle* had taken. Her shields were gone as were over seventy percent of her forward beams weapons. There was damage to her forward point defense systems as well, but right now, that didn't matter. The enemy missiles were approaching her from her aft and sides. Those systems had taken minimal damage, and she knew they would be more than enough to keep the current threat at bay given the enemy missiles' range.

"All available power to the engines!" Early shouted. "Get us out of here!"

The Federation super dreadnought poured on all it had as it altered course and made a run for Taskforce Hammer's chosen rallying point.

****

"Really?" Shannon frowned staring at the image of the alien super dreadnought in orbit around Cerebus VI. That hadn't been part of the plan. The plan had counted on the two alien super dreadnoughts to both be in the same section of the Cerebus system and for the *Castle* with her accompanying battleships to engage them both. Clearly, the pre-jump sensor intel had been wrong, and as usual, it was him and his crew who were going to be the ones to pay for it.

"Well, crap," Shannon muttered at last.

"That's your whole response, sir?" Williams nagged him. "That's a freaking alien super dreadnought out there ahead of us.

"Thank you, Williams," Shannon smirked, "but I can see that."

"Orders, sir?" Redder asked from the *Thrawn*'s helm.

"Keep us pointed at that planet, Redder," Shannon said as he thought about the fleet worth of alien battleships trying to catch up the *Thrawn* from behind her.

"We can't go head to head with that monster, sir," Williams protested.

"Oh ye of little faith, Williams." Shannon's lips parted in a grin. "Haven't you noticed that the big bad monster you're so terrified of hasn't opened up on us yet?"

Williams' mouth continued to work but no words came out as his features twisted in utter confusion.

"Close up of that thing on screen," Shannon ordered.

The image on the forward view screen zoomed in on the alien super dreadnought. The space around it was filled with tiny ships. Tiny being a relative term given that both the alien super dreadnought and the *Thrawn* herself were massive.

"What are those?" Redder asked before Williams could.

"Troop transports," Shannon explained. "She's unloading everything she's carrying or at least a good portion of it planet side. We've caught her with her pants down, gentlemen."

Redder laughed; Williams continued to turn another shade of pale.

"She can't shoot at us, gents," Shannon laughed. "Not without blowing away all the precious cargo she hauled her anyway. We've got it made."

Redder bobbed his head enthusiastically as he caught on to what Shannon was saying.

"Take us in, hard and fast, if you would, Mr. Redder," Shannon ordered with a smile.

"My pleasure, sir!" Redder shouted, his fingers dancing over the helm controls.

Just as Shannon predicted, the alien super dreadnought made no attempt to engage the *Thrawn* as she closed on Cerebus VI. The battleships pursuing her had to break away as she dived straight on into the planet's atmosphere. Unlike the *Thrawn*, those battleships and most vessels their size weren't designed to make a planet fall.

The *Thrawn's* shields lit up as atmospheric flames from her entry washed over them. They did no damage as this was what the *Thrawn* was designed to do. Once inside Cerebus VI's atmosphere, Redder leveled the *Thrawn* out.

"Where to now?" Redder asked.

Shannon snapped his fingers at Kinz, his sensor tech.

"There are already a great number of alien transports on the planet's surface, sir. The aliens appear to be targeting Cerebus VI's central city and landed waves of them around it on all sides," Kinz reported.

"Any place we can touch down inside the city?" Shannon asked.

"Negative, sir," Redder said with a frown. "The *Thrawn* is just too large for that."

Shannon sighed. "Right. How stupid of me to think things would be easy for once."

Calling up the data on the landing zones of the alien transports on the personal screen of his command chair's arm, Shannon looked it over. "They appear to be concentrating more on the city's northern side, so take us down there. Put us down behind them and give us a wide buffer so we have time to deploy before they can get their act together to come after us."

"Yes, sir!" Redder flashed him a feral smile and asked, "Light 'em up too?"

"All weapons, pick your targets and nail as many of those bastards as you can as we pass over them," Shannon said, nodding.

The alien transports weren't equipped for ship-to-ship combat, and that was something Shannon couldn't pass up the opportunity to take advantage of. The fact that they were essentially sitting ducks too only made him happier. The *Thrawn*'s railguns reduced half of the transports to nothing more than heaps of burning wreckage as the great ship howled above them, starting its descent.

"All hands, prepare for the crap to hit the fan!" Shannon shouted as Redder began the *Thrawn*'s landing process.

Shannon missed the days of leading the charge out of the *Thrawn*'s bay badly but comforted himself with the notion that he would be joining those troops rushing at the aliens outside her hull soon enough.

****

Major Gregory Henson was sweating inside his A-11 power suit. The mech was environmentally sealed and its internal temperature comfortable, but Henson still felt as if he were freezing to death with a cold fever as he waited on the bay doors in front of him to open. His squad, the Black Dogs, was composed for six of the A-11 mech units that the *Thrawn* carried. In total, there were two dozen A-11 mechs in her bays, but only his squad and one other, the Kill Cats, were presently being deployed. They were going to be running cover for the hundreds of soldiers who wore only standard battle armor that were about to go charging into the field behind them. In all, almost two-thirds of the ship's total ground combat strength were about to hit the ground running. Their orders were to push forward, secure as much area as they could, and prepare the way for the ship's APCs and tanks.

Having been on numerous drops, Henson knew exactly what was coming when the bay doors opened and it was sheer Hell. The only real hope of things being otherwise was the amount of damage the *Thrawn*'s railguns had done to the enemy troops on her way in. Henson had heard it was a lot and that the *Thrawn's* gun crews had trashed half of the transports waiting out there, but then one heard a lot of things, and not all of them tended to be true. Soldiers liked to talk things up. Some of them lived for it. Glory, honor, Gung-ho, and all that.

"You ready, sir?" Henson's second-in-command, Jeff asked over the squad's shared comlink and not the general one used by all of the *Thrawn's* forces.

"Are you implying that I have a choice, Lieutenant?" Henson snarled back at the younger man.

Jeff was a solid two decades younger than he was and had just turned twenty a month before. To look at the kid, when he wasn't suited up, Henson had a difficult time believing that Jeff was even that old. Jeff had no facial hair to speak of. Jeff blamed it on growing on in the Saturn colonies, but Henson wasn't buying it, well, at least not fully. The kid was a kid, and it was as simple as that. He, on the other hand, was getting too old for this crap, too fast. Henson had spent the last twelve years of his life in service to the Solar Federation armed forces, and even so, those nutjobs in the higher-up brass were trying to drive him into an honorable discharge just because he had hit the big forty. Lots of troops pushed on until they were close to their fifties and sometimes even later in life these days. All the new tech like the A-11 suits lessened the impact of age on one's combat effectiveness. Henson knew he would never, willing, retire. The Solar Federation Army was everything to him—mother, father, friend. He had nothing outside of the Army and didn't want anything else either. He did love these new A-11 power suits, though. They kicked arse and hard. Each suit stood nine to ten feet tall, depending on the pilot it was fitted for. Each suit was personalized to a great extent as well. Its pilot had a limited hand in its design and total control over the weapons the suit packed. His own suit had a tri-barrel right hand that could spray a whooping, three thousand rounds a minute in the enemy's ranks if set to continuous, stream fire. In addition, its left arm held a mounted flamethrower unit that could burn hot enough to cook the flesh off a person's bones on contact. A lot of troops opted for mini-missile launchers instead, whether arm- or shoulder-mounted; not Henson, though. He had experienced the value of having a secondary weapon like his flamethrower for close in defense. Missiles may be great for long range and sniping or laying down heavy fire on a distant enemy, but at the end of the day, as powerful as the A-11 suits were, they weren't tanks or even APCs. They could be overrun, toppled, and torn into by a determined foe. His flamethrower gave him a fantastic, close-in weapon to use anything that got through the kill zone of his tri-barrel. It had saved his life before, and Henson was sure it would again.

"On my mark!" Henson shouted over the comm. to the other members of the Black Dogs. "Let's do this thing!"

The *Thrawn*'s bay doors blew outwards, and the natural light of Cerebus VI's twin suns poured into the bay. The servo-motors of Henson's A-11 whined as he punched the suit into high gear and went lurching forward. He heard rounds pinging off the armor of his suit as the bright flashes of tracer rounds whizzed by him. The four mechs of the Black Dogs' squad formed a rough wedge outside the open bay doors and began to return fire at the enemy. Henson hadn't had any idea of what he and the rest of the *Thrawn*'s ground troopers would be facing. No one did. Not even Captain Shannon. There had been plenty of footage of the alien vessels relayed back to Taskforce Hammer by drones before it had ever made its jump into the Cerebus system. Now, Taskforce Hammer had seen those ships up close and personal, but still, there was no data at all on who or what was inside them.

Henson got his first look at the aliens who had invaded Cerebus VI as he whirled his mech about and brought up the tri-barrel of his right hand to fire on them. There were hundreds of them rushing towards the *Thrawn* in an attempt to hem in its forces before they could be deployed. The aliens stood between six and nine feet tall. Their bodies were impossibly thin and their sides covered from head to foot in what looked to be hundreds of tiny legs that extended from their body. In addition to those small legs, each alien had two almost normal arms and legs like a human would. Something seemed off about them, though

Shannon couldn't tell exactly what from this distance. At first glance, the aliens' sleekness made them seem fragile and weak. A longer look told the truth of the matter. They wore no clothes or armor. Their skin, or rather the natural, bug-like exoskeleton that acted as their skin, gleamed in the sunlight like metal. Henson had no doubt it was just as tough as it looked. Two antennas bristled and waved about wildly atop their heads and their eyes were giant, bulbous, monstrous orbs on the sides of their heads. They reminded Henson of Earth centipedes. The clicking, chattering noises of their movements could be heard even over the cacophony of gunfire that raged around Henson and the Black Dogs.

On the upside, their weapons were mostly outdated by Solar Federation standards. Many of the humanoid centipedes carried oddly curved rifles that were projectile weapons similar to Solar Federation machine guns. A few of the centipedes, however, carried twin pistols in their human-like hands instead of the rifles. The pistols were beam weapons. Their rate of fire was much slower, but the beams were deadly. Henson saw a mech from the Kill Cats squad take a hit from one. The beam burnt through the mech's armor as if it were butter, slicing through the chest of the mech and the human pilot inside it to erupt from the mech's back and continue onward. The mech toppled to the dirt with a heavy thud with both coolant fluids and human blood leaking from the hole the beam had burnt through it.

"Target the centipedes with the pistols!" Henson ordered over the general comm.

He followed his own order, his mech dropping to one knee, as his left hand steadied his right-hand tri-barrel. Henson fired aimed shot after aimed shot. The rounds from his first burst struck one of the centipedes full on in the chest. For a frightening second, Henson didn't know if the burst would be enough to take the bastard creature out. One round sparked harmlessly from its exoskeleton, the second round cracked it, but finally the third shattered the section it struck. Pieces of the ruptured exoskeleton spun away in the air as a disgusting, yellowish pus exploded from the centipede's wound. The creature gave a high-pitched screeched and staggered backwards before collapsing. Henson let out a sigh of relief as it did and moved on to his next target. He was limiting each burst he fired to three rounds to conserve ammo. It could be a very long time until he was able to head back onto the *Thrawn* for a fresh ammo pack.

Two more mechs fell; this time, one of them was a member of his Black Dogs, as the soldiers from the *Thrawn* charged passed the line of mechs, firing into the ranks of the centipedes as they ran. The heavy support guns that were mounted on turrets which extended from ports above the bay doors after the *Thrawn* had landed roared to life. They sprayed a continuous stream of armor-piercing rounds above the heads of the rushing soldiers into the ranks of the centipedes, laying waste to dozens and dozens of them. Centipede bodies crumpled under the fire of the support guns, some being blown completely apart while others had arms ripped from their shoulders and legs torn out from under them. The support guns did their job of driving the centipedes back very well.

In less than two minutes time, the ground was littered with the corpses of centipedes and humans alike, and the centipedes had been driven into a running retreat. The area around the *Thrawn* had been secured, and the commanders of the ground forces ordered for everyone to hold in place and await new orders.

Henson used the time to catch his breath and let his tri-barrel cool. Smoke drifted towards the sky from the mouths of its barrels. A two-second system check of his suit assured him that it had taken no serious damage from the centipedes' rifle fire. A few chips in the suit's paint job and the random, small dent from a lucky round were the worst he had been dealt.

"Black Dogs! Status!" he barked over the comm.

"Black Dog II, fully operational," Jeff reported.

"Black Dog IV, good to go, sir," Bones chimed in.

There would be no response coming from Black Dog III. Henson had watched Lucas die as one of the centipedes had burnt a hole through Black Dog III's faceplate with a shot from one of its pistols and its other had sent a bolt of energy slicing through Black Dog III's guts.

"Hold position for new orders," Henson told Jeff and Bones as he said an inward prayer for Lucas's departed soul.

****

The second attack from the centipedes came as a complete surprise. The grass was thick in the area where the *Thrawn* had touched down, and a line of small hills stretched over the distance between the ship and the alien transports just outside the planet's city. No one even noticed the centipedes until they were in yards of the ground force's main body. The creatures had somehow retracted their human-like appendages into their bodies and came slithering through the grass on the hundreds of tiny legs that covered their sides. A trooper named Buchanan had been the first to spot them. He had jerked the barrel of his rifle downwards to rake the back of one of the approaching centipedes as it charged him. His shots sparked off its armor, zinging away harmlessly until the creature had reached it. When it did, it reared up, lunging onto him. The tips of its small legs tore and stabbed at him. His armor saved him as he rolled his body, trying to twist away from the monster, but a lucky thrust by one the small legs punctured his throat. Blood exploded from the wound as Buchanan's screams turned into a nasty, gargling noise.

The other soldiers had instantly joined Buchanan in firing on the centipedes as soon as Buchanan had opened up on them. A handful of the centipedes died but not enough to matter as the things were suddenly within the ranks of the *Thrawn*'s ground forces. Utter chaos erupted. Here and there, a trooper died from friendly fire as someone would take a shot at one of the centipedes only to hit the soldier behind him as he either dropped or dodged out of the way.

"Fallback! Fallback!" an officer was shouting over the general comm., but there was nowhere to fall back to unless the ground forces completely withdrew onto the *Thrawn* and that was not an option.

The remaining mechs of Henson's Black Dogs and the Kill Cats were next to useless in the close-in melee. They were designed to hold or drive back the enemy at range, not combat fast-moving targets at their feet which darted about inside their own lines.

One of the centipedes slithered passed Henson's mech. He lunged forward, his mech's heavy foot ramming downwards onto the monster's back. The centipede's exoskeleton cracked and squirted yellow pus from the force and weight of the mech's foot crunching its body into the ground.

"Take that you little..." Henson started but didn't finish. Two more centipedes had seen what he had just done to their brother and opted to make him their primary target. They came scampering towards the feet of his mech like armored worms on speed. Henson couldn't swing his tri-barrel around in time to get a bead on them. One of the centipedes spouted razor-like mandibles as they extended from inside its jaws to stretch outwards from the sides of its face. They closed on the left foot of Henson's mech. Sparks flew as the mandibles slid up and down the mech's ankle, scraping away paint and flecks of metal armor. Henson activated his left-hand flamethrower, thrusting it towards the centipede on him. A geyser of flame washed over the creature, cooking it inside its own exoskeleton. Sickening popping noises cascaded along its length as its exoskeleton split, bursting apart, in several sections. The other centipede tried to withdraw, turning tail to run. As fast as it was though, the flames Henson sprayed at it still overtook it. The creature curled up into a ball, shrieking high-pitch death cries, as Henson continued to pour fire onto it.

"What in the devil are these things, sir?" Jeff screamed over the comm.

Henson whirled towards Jeff to see the man's mech grappling with one of the centipedes that had risen up to a height of nine feet. It stood face to faceplate with Jeff, the creature's mandibles snapping furiously at the head of Jeff's mech.

"Hold that thing still," Henson ordered Jeff, bringing his flamethrower into play against it. Henson knew that Jeff's suit could take the heat as he lit up the centipede. Flames washed over the centipede's backside, charring its armor-like exoskeleton. Its movements became erratic as the creature thrashed about in the hands of Jeff's mech. Then the fingers of Jeff's mech sunk through its weakened and cracking exoskeleton, and yellow pus oozed over them. Jeff gave a cry and flung the creature's corpse away from him.

"That was seriously messed up," Jeff rasped, holding his mech's hands up near his faceplate to stare at the yellow crap that slicked them. "I mean really, what the hell are they?"

"Aliens," Henson said as if that single word was supposed to explain everything and to him, it did.

"More bugs!" Jeff shouted, pointing at a trio of centipedes weaving a path through the grass towards where they stood.

"I got them!" Bones yelled, his mech stepping up beside them. With a clap of thunder, both of his mech's mounted shoulder launchers fired. Two mini-missiles streaked towards the trio of centipedes and detonated in their midst. The explosion crushed the centipedes as if they were rotten melons being smashed by a sledgehammer. Bits of their bodies went flying in every direction.

Henson started to congratulate Bones on his shot, but before he could, another centipede that had snuck up on them all from behind raced up the back of Bones' mech. Its mandibles latched onto the sides of one of Bones' shoulder-mounted launchers, biting down on it.

The world went white before Henson's eyes as Bones' mech became a blossoming ball of fire and flying shrapnel. Both his own mech and Jeff's were caught in the blast's shockwave and thrown from their feet. Henson's mech thudded hard onto its back, knocking the wind out of his lungs despite its internal cushioning against such impacts. Alarm klaxons were blaring in his ears as Henson fought to get air back into his lungs. He heard the sound of hundreds of pointed metal feet running up to and onto the body of his mech. His mech's normal sensor feeds were flickering in and out, which left him with only his own sight to rely on. He couldn't see the creature that was on top of him, but he knew it was on his lower body. Bringing his flamethrower up, he doused the stomach area and legs of his mech in flames. The centipede's pained shrieks let him know he had hit it.

Pushing the servos of his mech to their limit, Henson hauled himself up from the ground and got back onto his feet. There was no time to run a damage assessment to find out just how badly screwed he was. Instead, he whipped his head around, searching for Jeff. To his surprise, Jeff's mech was already on its feet, and Jeff had somehow managed to obtain a flamethrower unit of his own. It wasn't attached to his suit like Henson's was. In fact, it looked as if Jeff had torn it from the body of a downed mech that belonged to their sister squad, the Kill Cats. The weapon had to be awkward to operate given how Jeff was using it, but so far, the kid was doing a great job with it. The bodies of several more cooked centipedes were strewn about around his position, and he was busy frying another as Henson watched.

Then, with as little warning as it had begun with, the attack on the ground forces from the *Thrawn* suddenly stopped. The last remnants of scattered gunfire fell silent, and there were only the distant, clicking sounds of the centipedes on the retreat. Henson took the pause in the fighting as a chance to run a diagnostic on his mech. The results, while not as bad as he feared they would be, were not good. The joints of his left leg had taken damage. They were no longer one hundred percent reliable and stood the chance of locking up on him if he pushed them too hard. His right-hand tri-barrel was out of action. Its barrels had been bent by the force of him trying to catch himself during his fall. His suit's sensor suite had taken damage as well. The long-range portion still functioned fine, but up close, he was going to have to rely on his own eyesight and gut feelings. Being so close to the blast of Bones' mech exploding had weakened the integrity of his mech's armor but not overly much. All he could do was hope it would hold together.

"Glad that's over with," he heard Jeff sigh over the shared, squad specific comlink of the Black Dogs.

"Who said it's over?" Henson laughed. "Kid, it's just getting started."

****

Shannon was royally ticked off. He slammed a balled-up fist against the arm of his command chair as the reports of losses from his ground forces continued to come in. To Shannon, Williams seemed on the verge of being physically sick. His by the book, new XO just couldn't appear to truly cope with what had just happened. Yes, they had been walking into an unknown, up against aliens no one had even seen before, but they were the military of the Solar Federation, the ruling power of all known space. The amount of losses they had suffered just during their initial deployment on the planet were staggering- five out of eight A-11 mechs lost and nearly a full forty percent of their standard soldiers. The *Thrawn* was already running understrength for this mission from the start. A good portion of her normal holds had been given over to empty space so that they could rescue as many of Cerebus VI's citizens as they could should they be unable to take back the planet or hold its colony city. Nonetheless, they had to advance and do so now or things would only get worse.

Making a call from his gut, Shannon ordered, "Deploy the remainder of forces now in full. Order Ground Captain Jime to have a third of remaining strength take up defensive positions around this ship and to act as a reserve. All other forces are to press onward towards the city as soon as they are fully deployed."

"Sir, is that really a good idea?" Williams asked. "Perhaps we should contact the admiral to make her aware of what's happened here before we press on."

"I am aware that your job is to call me on things, Williams, and point out alternatives, but this is my ship, and those are my men dying out there. We press on, because if we don't, we'll lose whatever of an advantage we have left and will be overrun. As to what's happened out there, it's war, plain and simple. Losses are expected. We don't need to waste the admiral's time telling her that. Besides, I imagine she's rather busy just trying to stay alive herself. Taskforce Hammer inflicted some considerable damage to these alien freaks as we jumped in system but nowhere near enough to level the playing field. The odds are more against her up there than they are down here, even with our losses. Do I make myself clear?" Shannon concluded his rant.

"Crystal, sir." Williams gave him a reluctant nod.

"In the meantime, the *Thrawn* has a lot more to worry about than just those soldiers out there making it into the city. We're now in the same position those alien transports we blasted to shreds on our way in were. It's a pretty safe bet that we still have some time before that super dreadnought in orbit decides to start gunning for us, but that doesn't mean they might not have fighters or assault shuttles that it can send to do the job."

Some members of the bridge crew had rotated off duty or joined the ground forces since the *Thrawn* had touched down. The sensor station was now being manned by Lieutenant Angela Reed. Reed was one of the best sensor techs Shannon had at his disposal, and he was grateful to her eyes glued to the sensors' continually scrolling screens of new data.

As if reading his thoughts, she spoke up. "No sign of any small craft inbound so far, Captain," she told him. "And the alien super dreadnought continues to hold its position instead of shifting to target us."

"Thank God for that," Shannon cackled like a madman.

Williams stared at him as he thought he had gone insane.

"I'm fine, Williams," Shannon said. "Just enjoying the moment."

"As you say, sir," Williams shrugged.

Shannon figured his new XO didn't have the backbone to try to take away his command, but he knew even if Williams did, the crew of the *Thrawn* would never permit. Shannon had seen through too many fights just as tough as this one for some newbie to be allowed to oust him from power.

"Everybody keep alert and stay frosty," Shannon told his bridge crew. "We keep our cool, push on, and we might just live to tell our grandchildren about this someday."

****

Major Gregory Henson stood watching the last of the *Thrawn*'s ground forces disembark from her. Henson knew the captain was taking a big risk in pushing on like this. It was either take the city or die trying at this point. It remained unclear just how much of Cerebus VI's colony city had been overrun and occupied by the centipede-like aliens. The only way to find out was to fight through the alien troops and transports that stood between the *Thrawn* and the city.

The field techs had done all they could to repair his A-11 mech. Many of its systems were still compromised or at best shaky but they had truly done all they could for it without hauling it back onboard the ship for major repairs. Jeff's mech wasn't in that much better shape. They were the only two members of the Black Dogs squad that remained. As thus, they had joined with the surviving member of the Kill Cats to form a new squad now called Alpha Prime. Alpha Prime consisted solely of the three of them. The other two mech squads, the Diggers and the Banshees, were deployed now as well.

Harken, the commanding officer of the Banshees, had stopped by to touch base with him as the battle group as a whole got ready to move out. Harken was having a tough time believing the amount of damage the aliens had done to the Black Dogs and the Kill Cats. Henson hoped his overconfidence wouldn't get the man killed.

When word came down that Harken would be heading up all three mech squads as their overall C.O., Henson shuddered inside his A-11 and changed his prayer to asking God to protect them all.

Four APCs and two tanks had been unloaded from the ship. They would be the spearhead for the Federation ground forces as they pushed forward with the A-11 mechs acting as their support. The two tanks took point with the APCs fanning out behind and around them. The A-11 mechs ran alongside the APCs with the normal ground troopers following in a massive surge at the end of the procession.

The alien transport ships came into view up ahead. Henson feared the ships might have hidden weapons that would open fire and decimate them all at long range. No fire came from the transports, though. They appeared just as toothless as the captain had said they would be. Even so, waves upon waves of centipede warriors came charging to meet the tanks leading the *Thrawn*'s ground forces.

The main guns of the two tanks thundered. One alien transport rocked as a shell ripped open the side of its hull. Another alien transport vanished in a shower of fire and raining metal as it was hit by the shot from the second tank. The APCs joined in. Their top-mounted guns and rocket launchers spring to life, their fire raking over the transports that were scattered about the battlefield.

There was activity atop several of the transport ships. The centipede warriors were scurrying to erect what looked to be tripod-mounted weapons of some kind. Fire from the tanks and APCs continued to pick off transports at random. Henson didn't know if the crews of the heavy vehicles had spotted the new weapons that were being erected or not so he took action.

"This is Major Henson of Alpha Prime! All mechs, target the weapon crews getting into places on these ships!" he ordered as he downloaded a list of targets to all three mech squads.

"Major!" he heard Harken snap at him, but Harken didn't overrule him on the call he had made.

There would be time to worry about ticking Harken off later. Right now, what mattered was taking out those new weapons before they could be brought into play. The field techs had managed to get his tri-barrel partially active again. It couldn't lay down the thick rain of fire it once had, but it could still deliver aimed shots at a distance. Rising his right-hand tri-barrel, Henson took aim at a group of centipede warriors to his left. Firing single shots, Henson blew the head from one of the centipede's shoulders and put two rounds into the chest of another. Jeff and Alex, the last of the Kill Cats, joined in with him. Jeff's shoulder-mounted launcher spat a missile directly into the body of the weapon the centipede had been trying to ready. The explosion covered the entire top of the alien transport, ripping a hole in it before the rounds from Alex's heavy machine even reached their target.

One of the groups of centipedes at least had managed to complete the set of whatever kind of weapon they had been struggling to bring online. They swiveled it around on its tripod base to take aim at one of the two Federation tanks. Bright purple energy danced along the weapon's extended barrel, coalescing into a blazing orb at its end. The weapon spat the ball of energy towards the Federation tank. It struck the tank in its side. The energy of the orb spread out over the armor of the tank, crackling and dancing over it, shorting out systems as it went, until the tank blossomed into an explosion that rocked the ground beneath the feet of Henson's mech.

"Holy!" Henson heard Jeff yell.

"That thing just took out a tank in one shot!" Alex chimed in.

"Kill it now!" Henson ordered, swinging the body of his mech around towards the transport that the functional weapon had been completed on top of. His tri-barrel boomed in rapid succession as he fired shot after shot at the centipede crew surrounding the weapon. Half of his hurried shots missed, but those that struck their targets sent centipedes flying from their feet, exoskeletons cracked and leaking yellow pus. One centipede took a shot to its shoulder that hurled it from the top of the transport it stood on. Another died instantly as its head developed a hole in its center and was jerked backwards with enough force to snap its neck, in addition to the already fatal injury it had been dealt. Still another lost one of its two human-like arms as one of Henson's shots separated the limb from the alien's body near its shoulder joint. Jeff had switched over to his mech's tri-barrel mowing down the remaining centipedes. Alex had been unable to join in. The first wave of charging centipede warriors had closed in now, and Alex was doing her best to hold them back from him and Jeff.

Alex's A-11 mech didn't sport the fixed-on weapons that those of the two Black Dogs did. Instead, she carried a powerful M-124, anti-personnel weapon. It was a heavy machine gun, the kind normally mounted onto an APC or tank. Alex was using it as a hand weapon though, thanks to the strength of her mech. The M-124 was belt-fed from a pack she carried on her mech's back. Human-finger sized, spent rounds flew from its side as the huge gun chattered, hosing the advancing centipedes with a continuous stream of high-velocity rounds. Alex mowed down dozens of the centipede warriors, sweeping the M-124 back and forth in a wide arc of fire. For every centipede that fell, though, there was another to take its place.

One of the centipedes sporting the twin energy pistols, that a fourth of their number carried instead of rifles, took aim at Alex. Henson tried to scream a warning over the comm., but it was too late. The centipede went to work on Alex like an old west gunfighter determined to riddle its enemy full of holes. One energy bolt after another sliced through Alex's A-11 mech. Alex's mech took a half-dozen good shots, reeling about wildly, before the centipede decided to end its game and put a shot straight through Alex's faceplate.

Having finished the gun crew atop the transport, Henson watched Alex die. He blamed himself for it. With Harken dead, he was now Alpha Prime squad's C.O. and should have been paying more attention to what was coming at his own squad than trying protect the *Thrawn*'s heavier forces. A good C.O. did both not just one at the expense of the other and now Alex was dead because of his screw up.

With a rage-filled battle cry, Henson shifted the aim of his tri-barrel and started blasting away at the approaching centipedes. Rounds from the projectile rifles the bulk of the centipede warriors carried pinged against the armor of his mech. They gouged at its metal and stripped away its paint but did little else. Henson saw one of the centipedes packing the twin energy pistols taking aim at him and put a round through its skull that splattered brain matter and exoskeleton fragments into the air behind it. The centipede collapsed, dead, tripping up several others charging in his direction.

Jeff was holding his own. The kid had talent. He fired his tri-barrel in controlled bursts. Each one he fired sent a centipede warrior to Hell. Jeff had grown up fast in the heat of combat, Henson thought and laughed as he took a shot at a centipede warrior that had retracted its human-like arms and legs up into its body and dropped to the ground. It skittered towards him on hundreds of tiny legs as his bullet dug a fist-sized hole in it. Yellow pus exploded from the wound, but the thing kept coming. Henson had to put two more rounds into the thing before it finally gave up its ghost.

"Look out!" Jeff howled at him.

Henson whirled about to come face to face with a nine-foot-tall centipede warrior. As their eyes met, it thrust a spear into and through the guts of his A-11 mech. He felt the spear piece his body, cutting through it, as the spear's tip emerged from the backside of his mech's body. Henson coughed and then blinked. When his eyes opened, slashes of blood spotted the interior of his faceplate. The centipede warrior twisted the spear around inside him, ensuring his death. With a grim smile, Henson raised his right-hand tri-barrel level with the centipede's head. "See you in

Hell," he croaked as he fired, and the centipede warrior's head was reduced to pulp by the point-blank shot.

****

Admiral Early took stock of the regrouped remnants of Taskforce Hammer. The *Thrawn* was of course gone. It had made planetfall on Cerebus VI where the troops it carried fought to re-secure the colony there, or at worst, rescue whatever civilians, if any, that remained alive. Its firepower would be sorely missed in the next engagement with the alien fleet which still held control of the system. However, six of the taskforce's seven battleships were present and mostly undamaged. Only one had been lost in the taskforce's headlong retreat to its rallying point on the far side of the Cerebus system. Her destroyer screens were pretty gone. Taskforce Hammer had entered the system with twelve destroyers and now only three remained and one of them was damaged so badly, it was leaking atmosphere from its portside despite its crew's efforts to seal off that section of the ship.

The alien fleet had for the time being opted to regroup itself, and as thus, leave Taskforce alone with time to lick its wounds. That wouldn't last, and Admiral Early knew it. Sooner or later, most likely sooner, the aliens would come at Taskforce Hammer head on. They had the numbers to accept heavy losses and still crush every ship she had at her command.

She needed a plan and she needed one fast. Waiting for the aliens to come to her might prove a fatal mistake. She lacked the firepower to on the offensive without the guns of the *Thrawn*, though. Her ship, the *Castle*, may be a Federation super dreadnought, but it had suffered heavy damage destroying one of the alien super dreadnoughts that had been waiting on Taskforce Hammer when it arrived. Most of the *Castle*'s damage was contained to its forward sections. That meant the giant ship was massively vulnerable in a head-on attack.

The *Castle* and all the ships of Taskforce Hammer had lost long-range communications upon entering the Cerebus system. Her techs told her that the alien ships were emitting some type of signal jamming that they just couldn't find a means of countering. That had left her with only dispatching drones as her sole hope of contacting the rest of the Solar Federation to inform the counsel. She had done so, but there was little chance of her getting any kind of rushed reinforcements sent to her aid or even a reply before the alien fleet came at her taskforce.

The more she weighed her few options, the more it became clear that she was going to have to go on the offensive. So far, only some of the alien warships had proven tactically, faster than those of Taskforce Hammer. And the *Castle*, even in her damaged state, was just as fast her alien counterpart. The key to it all might hinge on taking out the second alien super dreadnought.

Yes, the vast numbers, in comparison to her own, of alien battleships and destroyers were deadly, but with the super dreadnought gone, Taskforce Hammer's chances of survival soared upwards. The question was how to eliminate the monster-sized vessel in orbit around Cerebus VI while keeping her own losses to a minimum. Try as she might, she could only conjure up two ways of doing so. The first was to contact the *Thrawn* and have Captain Shannon abandon his men on the planet's surface. The *Thrawn* was in a near-perfect position to trap the alien super dreadnought between it and her own ship, the *Castle*. The *Castle* could be the hammer and the *Thrawn*, the anvil. Their combined firepower would be able to overpower the alien super dreadnought. There were numerous issues with that plan, though. It would require the *Castle* and the other ships of Taskforce Hammer to fight a path to the planet to meet the *Thrawn*. That in and of itself wasn't that difficult and could be done. Convincing Shannon to leave his men behind though was unlikely. She had known Shannon a long time, and despite all his shortcomings as an officer and leader by her standards, lack of honor wasn't among them. The other shot at taking out the alien super dreadnought was one she would never contemplate under different circumstances. She could order two to three of the battleships at her disposal to make the ultimate sacrifice by ramming their ships down the alien super dreadnought's throat.

Frowning, Admiral Early wiggled about in her command chair. She had to make a call and do so soon. The longer she waited, the more dangerous things become. There was no certainty that more alien ships wouldn't jump in system. The odds were already vastly against her, and if the aliens brought more forces to bear against her, it would be over no matter what she did.

"Admiral," the voice of a young officer grabbed her attention. Admiral Early looked up from her command chair into the green eyes Lieutenant Chalker. Chalker had taken over the communications station a few minutes earlier as part of the bridge crew rotated off duty. Admiral Early liked Chalker. The woman was full of a determination and energy that reminded her of herself in her younger days. Chalker was a capable officer with a bright future ahead of her assuming that Taskforce Hammer made it out of the Cerebus system alive.

"What is it?" Admiral Early asked.

"Incoming message from Captain Shannon, ma'am," Chalker told her. "I figured you want to take it personally."

Chalker handed her an earpiece that Early shoved in her ear before speaking over the encrypted channel to the *Thrawn*. "Early here. Go ahead, Shannon."

"It's good to hear your voice, too," Shannon answered and she could imagine the lopsided, sarcastic grin on his smug features.

"I heard about the losses you've taken," Admiral Early growled. "Neither one of us have time for games right now, Shannon. What do you want?"

She could sense his surprise at her words. "Have you now? Heard about our losses, I mean?"

"Your new XO Williams uploaded a data package of the details to Taskforce Hammer's net some time ago."

"I guess I'll be having some words with Williams in the near future. He was under orders not to bother you."

"He didn't, but you are, Shannon," Admiral Early snapped. "Get to the point."

"Right," Shannon said, "We're picking up some really weird energy readings in Cerebus VI's colony city. The readings indicate something huge is powering up in there. I was hoping you might have some idea what that something might be."

"And how would I know that?" Admiral Early grunted.

"Well, you are in a better position to get accurate scans of the planet's surface than we are down here. The centipedes have bloody jammers everywhere."

"Centipedes?" she repeated the word. "That's what you're calling them?"

"That's what my men are calling them. These aliens look a lot like centipedes okay? It's as good of a name as any."

"I see," Admiral Early sighed. "I can't help you, though. The centipedes, as you call them, are jamming us up here, too. We've lost contact with Command back home."

"Crap," Shannon muttered. "So we're on our own then?"

"We always knew we would be," Admiral Early reminded him. "Taskforce Hammer is made up of every ship the Solar Federation had that was remotely within striking distance of the Cerebus system. You bet Command is assembling a larger fleet as we speak, but it'll never reach this system in time to make any difference for us."

"I assume you dispatched drones," Shannon half-asked.

"I did," Admiral Early sighed. "They made it out of the system, free and clear, so Command should at least know just how badly we screwed we are."

"Somehow, I don't find that very comforting."

"Tell me more about these strange power readings you're getting," Admiral Early ordered.

"Not much to tell really. They're powerful. I mean that in the sense that if you took the drives from all the ships of Taskforce Hammer and multiplied them tenfold, you might be getting close to the level we're picking up down here."

That's insane, she thought before she spoke again. "Are you sure the readings you're getting are accurate?"

"One hundred percent sure," Shannon said grimly.

"The only thing that would take that much power..." she started.

"Is a planet killer weapon of some type," Shannon finished for her.

"Can you stop it?" Admiral Early asked.

"We haven't even been able to get into the city yet," Shannon reminded her.

As if he sensed what was coming next, Shannon said, "I am not leaving my men out there to die. Enough people are going to die anyway, even if I am able to recall them and withdraw before whatever the aliens are powering up comes online."

"Then I strongly suggest you find a way into the city and stop whatever is going on there, Captain." Admiral Early rubbed at the sharp pain that was beginning in her temples. It had been a long time since she had a stress headache, but there was no mistaking that one was hitting her now. "Contact me again when you have."

Ending the transmission, Admiral Early handed the small, personal comm. device back to Lieutenant Chalker. "Thank you," she told the young officer again. "I need you to get me Captain Desard and Captain Payne. Patch the two of them through to my ready room. I'll handle things from there. XO, you have the conn."

Admiral Early got out of her command chair and started for her ready room but stopped, turning to Chalker again. "And find me some painkillers," she ordered. "Bring them to my ready room ASAP."

"Yes, Admiral," Lieutenant Chalker nodded her. "Right away, ma'am."

****

Jeff found himself in command of all the surviving mechs of the *Thrawn*'s ground forces. They had merged into one, over-strength squad, now called Beta Prime. There were six mechs total including his own. The ground forces' losses had continued to be staggering, but they had overrun the alien transports between them and Cerebus VI's colony city.

Both tanks had been destroyed in the battle with the alien transports and their surrounding centipede warriors. Only two of the *Thrawn*'s armored personnel carriers remained functional and combat ready. The heavier of the two led the way ahead of Jeff's mechs and the hundreds of infantry troopers who had survived. The other APC brought up the rear.

Major Henson's death had taken a heavy toll on Jeff. He had thought the old man was immortal. To see the major taken out and gutted by an alien spear was terrifying. Even more so was the fact that he was now in command. Jeff had never wanted command. He wasn't career military like the old man had been. He just wanted to do his time, serve, and get the hell out of the Solar Federation's armed forces with a nice nest egg set aside for his future. Yet here he was, playing a role he wasn't cut out for, with the lives of the other five mech pilots weighing heavily on his shoulders.

Jeff had hoped that the captain might order a withdrawal after the battle with the alien transports. The *Thrawn*'s ground forces were hardly in any shape to continue their push towards Cerebus VI's colony city, but that was exactly what the captain had ordered them to do.

Dialing up an image of the city's wall less than a mile ahead, Jeff could see that the centipedes had laid waste to it. The city's outer wall was broken through in numerous areas, and the bodies of the city's security forces mixed on the ground with the corpses of centipede warriors. The city's defenders seemed to have put a good fight as they died, not that it mattered.

Major Martin Reed, aboard one of the two remaining APCs, was now in overall command of the remaining ground forces. The major was using the APC's as a mobile command center and holding back near the rear the battle group's overall formation. Jeff didn't blame the major for playing it as safe as he could. There weren't many officers of rank left to speak of, and they needed someone like Reed to oversee and coordinate the assault on the city.

Jeff listened to Major Reed's voice as he barked orders over the group's shared comm-net.

"Tango 1," that was the call sign of the lead APC, "clear the way through the rubble at these coordinates," Reed ordered as Jeff watched the data on the coordinates scrolling across the interior of his mech's faceplate. "Beta Prime Leader, have your mechs follow Tango 1 in. Lay down suppressive fire at anything that comes your way until the infantry units are able to join up with you. Then, push straight on into the city."

"Roger that," Jeff echoed Tango 1's commander.

Tango 1 gunned its engines and plowed through the rumble of a downed section of the city's wall. Jeff led his mechs in after it. Tango 1's topside, mounted gun turret was blazing away at a group of centipede warriors in the city's street as Jeff's mech came stumbling over the piles of debris that the APC's charge hadn't cleared. Darrin and Shanna were on his heels as Alan, Zachary, and Lancaster spread out behind them.

The high-velocity rounds from Tango 1's gun made short work of the small group of centipede warriors splattering the street with the yellow pus that served as their blood. For a moment, Jeff allowed himself to believe that pushing into the city was going to be easy. They were approaching the enemy from the rear, and there was no sign of the bulk of the centipede's forces. That hope was shattered though as something akin to a Federation RPG came flying into the driver's side of Tango 1. The blast from the alien RPG lifted Tango 1 from the ground as it ripped the entire front of the heavy vehicle into twisted metal.

"Get down!" Jeff screamed over the comm-net.

His mech dropped to one knee as his eyes scoured the windows of the building along the street trying to locate where the alien RPG had been fired from. The mech's limited, targeting AI pinged the location of the alien sniper before Jeff saw him. Jeff jerked his tri-barrel around to engage the sniper, but before he could get off a shot, the sniper was dead. A twenty-foot section of the floor of the building where the sniper had been hiding was vaporized by a mini-missile fired from one the shoulder launchers mounted onto Darrin's mech.

Jeff allowed himself a smile. He had no time to congratulate Darrin on his shot, though. The sniper had apparently just been meant to slow the headlong rushing Solar Federation forces down. Angry shrieking and the clattering of countless tiny legs erupted from the depths of the city as a vast wave of centipede warriors emerged, charging towards Beta Prime's position.

Alan, Zachary, and Lancaster were already pouring fire into the centipedes' ranks as Jeff's mech rose to its full height. Tri-barrels and mini-missiles decimated the centipedes' front lines filling the street with their mangled corpses.

"Orders, sir?" Darrin shouted at him.

"We hold here," Jeff spat. "Whatever it takes."

"Whatever it takes," Darrin repeated, though Jeff didn't know if the man was trying to assure him or himself.

The mechs of Beta Prime dug in and stood their ground. The centipedes were mostly coming at them like the insects they appeared to be. The bulk of the warriors had retracted their human-like arms and legs up into their bodies and came skittering along the street on the hundreds of tiny legs that ran the lengths of the sides of their bodies. This gave them the advantage of speed but took away their ability to attack until they closed to melee range. Jeff understood the tactic. He and the mechs under his command hammered the centipedes with everything they had. The city street was slick with yellow pus within a matter of seconds, but still the centipedes came.

Not all of the centipede warriors had joined in the mad charge, though. Those that held back struck at the mechs of Beta Prime, trying to draw their fire and inflict what damage they could before their brothers entered the kill zone around the mechs.

"RPG!" Darrin shouted even as the sensor suite of Jeff's mech warned him of the inbound projectile. Darrin and Jeff flung themselves in opposite directions trying to dodge it. The RPG streaked passed them. Poor Alan never stood a chance. The RPG struck his mech in the dead center of its chest. The mech and Alan with it blew apart in a shower of spinning metal bits and blood. The shockwave from the blast put Zachary and Lancaster on their butts, leaving only Shanna to continue firing at the charging centipede warriors who grew closer with each second.

The tri-barrel of Shanna's mech clicked empty. Jeff scurried to his feet as he watched Shanna pop the weapon from her suit and long vibro-blades slid outwards from their internal sheathes on the tops of her mech's arms. With a berserker-like battle cry, Shanna kicked her mech into high gear, sprinting forward to wade into the centipedes. Her blades sliced and diced centipede warriors by the dozens. A swipe from one of her blades cut one of the centipedes in half along its middle from head to tail. Another took a centipede's head from its shoulders to send it bouncing along the street leaving splashes of yellow pus in its wake. Shanna speared one centipede with a blade, lifting it high into the air, before she flung it in the ranks of those behind it. Watching Shanna was like watching an ancient Samurai warrior in the days of old as she gutted one foe before whirling about to slash another. She was like a legend come to life.

Jeff and the others rose to lay down cover fire for her. A burst from Jeff's tri-barrel ravaged the back of a centipede as it to slither around Shanna to come at her from her flank. Darrin emptied his remaining missiles at the distant group of centipedes, driving them back while Zachary popped his own mech's blades and staggered forward to join Shanna in the sea of carnage she had created.

By now, the infantry units of the *Thrawn*'s ground forces had entered the battle. They hung back, staying well clear of the charging centipede warriors and the chaotic melee. The fire from the weapons swept the street clean of the last of the surviving centipede who had been charging forward.

No one saw the next RPG until it hit. Jeff had heard his mech's sensor suite warn him of the projectile, but even those sensors hadn't been able to pinpoint its trajectory. The RPG nailed Shanna, ending her dance of death. Its blast took Zachary with her. Their two mechs vanished in a blossoming ball of raging heat and flames.

"Shanna!" Jeff heard Darrin cry out and knew Darrin had just lost it. The two of them had been an item aboard the *Thrawn* since the toned, sexy goddess of death had transferred aboard two months before.

Darrin sprinted by Jeff, making a b-line for what was left the distant centipede forces who in the process of a full out retreat. The tri-barrel of Darrin's mech spun, spraying a continuous stream of rounds at the centipedes. Darrin dropped several of them before one carrying the deadly, twin energy pistols the aliens used as their primary means of combating Jeff's mech squad, cut him down. The centipede's first shot went low but still managed to blow out the knee of Darrin's mech. Darrin's mech hit the ground rolling. When it stopped, Darrin instantly tried to get to his feet. As he did so, the centipede finished him a headshot that left a cantaloupe-sized hole burnt through Darrin's faceplate and the backside of his mech's head.

Jeff shook away the pain he felt at watching another member of his squad die. The *Thrawn*'s ground forces were finally making headway at getting into the depths of the city and that was where his focus needed to be.

Waving an arm to urge what was left of Beta Prime on, Jeff shouted, "We got these bastards on the run! Let's not give them a chance to regroup!"

****

The talk with Captain Desard and Captain Payne had gone as well as it could. They had agreed to her plan much more quickly than she had believed they would. It spoke volumes about their sense of duty and honor. Still, Admiral Early couldn't help feeling the guilt that came with ordering them and their entire crews to give up their lives so that Taskforce Hammer might have a shot at changing the tide of the battle in the Cerebus system. The plan was for all the remaining ships of Taskforce Hammer to chance an in-system jump which would allow them to bypass most of the alien fleet and put them in a position to go after the alien super dreadnought in orbit around Cerebus VI. Jumping so close to a planet came with a lot of risk. Re-entering normal space inside of the planet's gravity well or emerging directly into a collision with the alien ships screening the super dreadnought would be bad to put it mildly. There was no other course to victory, though. Of that, Admiral Early was sure.

She paced the bridge of the *Castle* as she awaited the completion of the jump calculations. Admiral Early had pulled Chief Les from engineering to plot the jump. She didn't trust anyone else to do it. Les might be her chief engineer and not officially an astro-navigator, but the man was a mathematical genius. In the beginning of his career in the Solar Federation Navy, Les had suffered a severe brain injury saving the lives of several of his crewmates. Parts of his cerebral lobes had been replaced with top of the line tech that made him the closest thing to a living computer in the history of the Federation.

Admiral Early stopped her nervous pacing as she realized Les was staring at her.

"The jump is plotted, ma'am," he informed her in his usual emotionless tone. The same implants that gave him such an edge at his job as chief of engineering, and allowed him to make the staggering calculations of jumps like the one he had just finished, also left him cold and unable to truly show emotions.

"Thank you, Chief." Admiral Early smiled. "You may return to your post now."

Chief Les gave her a sharp nod and left the bridge. Her helmsman, Wiggins, the best pilot she had aboard the *Castle*, took control of the helm again.

"All ships of Taskforce Hammer," Admiral Early spoke over the fleet wide channel, "prepare to jump on my mark."

She glanced around the bridge. All of her bridge crew were putting on brave, professional faces, but she knew deep down, that each and every one of them was just as worried about this jump as she was.

"Let's go show these bugs that they picked the wrong race to tangle with," she said off comm. to her crew.

Reopening the fleet wide channel, she ordered, "All ships, jump!"

The *Castle*, the seven battleships, and last destroyers of Taskforce Hammer blinked out of existence.

They all exploded out of their individual jump points close to Cerebus VI a fraction of a second later except for one destroyer, the *Nimz*. Only God in heaven knew where that ship ended up. The *Hearldson,* one of the seven battleships, burst from its jump point, plunging into one of the alien battleships. Both it and the enemy vessel died instantly in an explosion of fire and white light.

Taskforce Hammer's losses were far less than they had any right to be. Admiral Early thanked God and Chief Les's mathematical genius for that. Captain Desard's ship, the *Hellbender,* and Captain Payne's ship, the *Furious*, pushed their drives beyond the red-line as they charged headlong towards the alien super dreadnought. Its surprised crew tried their best to react in time to make a difference. Missiles slid from the alien super dreadnought's tubes and bright, point defense energy beams blasted outwards to meet the two battleships.

Admiral Early watched as the *Hellbender* and the *Furious* took a vicious beating. Their shields failed and both battleships took heavy damage. Not enough to stop them from their goal, though. They plunged into the alien super dreadnought like oversized missiles. The *Hellbender* died first, taking the super dreadnought's shields with it as it broke apart from its impact with them. The battleship's shredded wreckage continued onward, each piece of debris stabbing into the alien super dreadnought's hull like spinning knives. Explosions rippled over the entire structure of the monstrous alien ship before the *Furious* ended it. With its shields gone and the alien super dreadnought already reeling, the *Furious* rammed into its central mass.

"Brace for impact!" Admiral Early shouted, anticipating the shockwaves from the alien super dreadnought's death. The massive ship blew apart like an exploding moon.

The alien ships screening it took the brunt of the shockwaves, but the ships of Taskforce Hammer felt them, too. They were powerful enough to rock even the *Castle*, sending Admiral Early staggering to collapse into her command chair. The *Castle*'s already weakened forward defenses simply weren't up to the job for blocking the shockwaves. Several stations blew out across the bridge around. The *Castle*'s sensor tech leaped from his chair, his station a mess of sparking wires and open flames, with the sleeves of his uniform ablaze. Others of the bridge crew took bruises as they were jarred into the consoles in front of them or flung from their seats to the bridge's floor.

The *Hellbender* and the *Furious* had done their job. The alien super dreadnought was out of play. Now, it was up to the *Castle* and the other ships of Taskforce Hammer to finish what they had started by wiping out the alien battleships and destroyers in the system.

Admiral Early righted herself in her command chair. She quickly ran the fingers of her right hand through her hair to help her center herself and then started barking orders. The lesser alien vessels were already closing in on her ships and opening fire on them.

"All ships of Taskforce Hammer, pick your targets and fire at will!" she yelled over the fleet-wide comm.

****

With the loss of Tango 1, Major Reed's APC, Tango 2, had taken the lead. Jeff and the remaining mechs of his Beta Prime squad jogged alongside it, covering its flanks. The *Thrawn*'s infantry troopers kept pace as best as they could behind the APC and mechs. Beta Prime really wasn't a squad anymore. Jeff and Lancaster piloted the only two surviving mech units. Jeff took Tango 2's right while Lancaster covered the vehicle's left side.

The centipedes hadn't made any real effort to hold against them again. There had been a few skirmishes here and there as Major Reed kept them all pushing forward into the city but nothing serious. The skirmishes basically amounted to small groups wandering into their path from side streets or stumbling onto a few dozen stragglers from the centipedes' main force.

They were approaching the center of Cerebus VI's colony city. Jeff couldn't help but wonder where all the civilians were. Sure, there were bodies scattered and rotting all over the streets but not anywhere near enough to account for the city's population. Were they holed up in their homes, afraid to come out even with Solar Federation forces marching up the streets, or had the centipedes somehow managed to kill them all before the *Thrawn* ever reached the planet? Thinking about the colony's civilian population proved to be a mistake. Jeff found his gaze lingering on the worst of the bodies in the streets. Mothers and fathers with their children squeezed tight, all of them charred to little more than bones. One corpse, clearly male, lay at the edge of the street, his body riddled with holes from the projectiles of the centipedes' rifles, and from where he lay looked to have been almost within reach of the alleyway he must have been trying to escape into when he was gunned down. Another corpse was that of a woman with a single cauterized wound in the center of her chest between her breasts. Her mouth was twisted in the shriek of an attempted scream. The bolt of energy that surely must have melted her heart had killed her instantly. Yet another body of a young woman, directly in Jeff's path, must have been overtaken by the skittering centipedes. Her flesh was chewed upon, and it was clear that the creatures had made a snack out of her. She was Jeff's breaking point. He felt vomit and bile rise up in his throat. Through sheer willpower, he swallowed it back, averting his eyes from the woman's body. Warm tears well up in his eyes that he blinked away as he shook his head to clear it and find his focus.

"Hey, Lancaster," Jeff called over the closed channel of the Beta Prime squad comlink.

"What is it, boss?" Lancaster answered.

"Where do you think all the people are?" Jeff asked.

A heartbeat ticked by before Lancaster responded. "All around you, sir. You not seeing what I am seeing?"

"Oh, I'm seeing it alright," Jeff kept his voice calm and professional as best he could. "I know there are a lot of corpses out here, but wasn't this colony supposed to have around three hundred million residents?"

"Not sure I am reading you, sir," Lancaster said.

"I'm saying we're not seeing enough bodies to account for anywhere near that amount," Jeff explained.

"It's a big city, sir," Lancaster sighed, "Maybe the bulk of them made a stand somewhere else."

"Could be," Jeff agreed though he didn't really believe it. "I'm just saying I think we're missing something here."

"Your suit has taken a lot of damage, hasn't it?" Lancaster asked.

"For sure," Jeff laughed darkly. "Why?"

"I've been picking up an odd radiological reading for the last few blocks. My suit's AI doesn't seem to think it's harmful, but we both know that AI's can be wrong," Lancaster pointed out.

Jeff tried to check his suit's own data about the radiation only to find it had none. His AI was mostly offline and his sensor suite barely functional. "Dang it," he cursed to himself.

"Major Reed hasn't commented on it yet," Lancaster told him. "Could be his APC is as messed up as our suits, or maybe the guys inside Tango 2 have just been too busy to notice."

"Or maybe he has noticed and opted not tell the rest of us about it," Jeff countered. "Those poor ground pounders behind us don't have any protection against it whatever it may be."

"Hey, we're ground pounders, too," Lancaster chuckled, trying to break the tension.

"Yeah, but we're ground pounders inside sealed, armored killing machines," Jeff said and glanced over his shoulder at the infantry troopers behind them. The troopers were keeping pace and moving along like the professionals they were, but some of them did appear to be on the verge of collapse from more than just the exhaustion that came with their job.

"Holy crap," Jeff muttered. "What if this radiation was stronger before we got here? If it was and has only now leveled out to close to norms, it could be why we're not seeing survivors from the colony."

"Well, I ain't calling the major on it," Lancaster said, his tone a mixed mess of anger and fear. "If he knows about it and didn't tell the rest of us, you can be sure he had a reason for doing so."

"Like not having our infantry bolt?" Jeff said and regretted it. His brain struggled for a way to take his foot out of his mouth and change the subject. He was saved by a flash of light up ahead that lit the dimness of the twilight sky. The planet's twin suns were in the process of setting, but whatever had happened ahead of their advancing column was brighter than both of them put together at their peak.

"Mercy!" Jeff heard Lancaster yell as the light washed over them.

The light didn't dim or fade away. It remained and kept the sky bright above them.

"What the hell is that?" Lancaster asked him, his voice trembling.

"No clue," Jeff answered honestly "No clue at all."

Suddenly, Major Reed's voice interrupted their conversation. "All units, pick up the pace. Push it forward, ladies!"

Tango 2's engines revved as the APC's speed increased and it darted forward like a bullet. Jeff and Lancaster had to push their mechs to the max to even attempt keeping up with it. The infantry were now running full out but falling behind even so.

Jeff glanced up at the light in the sky with each step he took. He scrolled the visual options of his suit still available to him until he hit on a shielded mode that allowed him to see the sky more clearly. Amid the overall, nearly blinding sea of light in the sky, there was a single almost wave-shaped center to it. What the devil it was, he still didn't have a clue, but it was scary looking as the devil himself.

Tango 2 rounded a corner at the end of the street the column was advancing along. Instantly, the APC's topside gun erupted. It thundered out a steady pulse of automatic fire. Jeff and Lancaster rounded the corner in its wake. The turn opened in a vast, wide-open area of the city that appeared to have been cleared out by the centipedes. There was rubble everywhere covering the street and ground among the smoking leveled out remains of the buildings that had once stood there. Somewhere around two hundred centipede warriors stood between Tango 2 and what appeared to be a tringle-shaped machine that pulsated with glowing energy that danced over its sides from top to bottom.

The centipede warriors made no effort to dodge the fire hitting them from Tango 2's primary weapon. It cut them down by the dozens. They did return fire, though. One centipede launched an RPG at Tango 2. The APC's driver swerved hard as it bounced through the rubble beneath its wheels. The RPG exploded where it struck the spot the APC had been only a half second before. The force of the blast was still enough to roll Tango 2. The vehicle, already having trouble moving because of the rubble and well into a too-sharp turn, was lifted from the ground and hurled sideways. It crashed onto its side then it top, then its side again before finally coming to a stop. A second RPG finished it as it impacted with the vehicle's underside and turned it into a mess of flying shrapnel.

Jeff and Lancaster threw themselves flat to avoid the spinning debris. Lancaster was back on his feet first, his tri-barrel roaring as he raked the closest of the centipedes with a continuous stream of high-velocity rounds.

"What is that thing, sir?" Lancaster screamed even as he continued to hose the centipedes with his tri-barrel.

Jeff had no answer so he kept his mouth shut. The tringle-shaped machine was at least half the size of the *Thrawn*. It stretched across the entire heart of the colony city and reached upwards into the sky above it. It was the source of the light that lit up the night sky, and Jeff wagered it was the source of the odd radiological readings Lancaster had told him about, too.

The infantry troopers caught up with them as one of the centipede warriors carrying the deadly, twin energy blasters they used to combat mechs with caught Lancaster with a well-aimed shot. The bolt of energy it fired at Lancaster hit his mech's power-core dead on. Lancaster's mech didn't explode though, at least not outwardly. Instead, its explosion was contained inside the suit itself. Jeff watched in horror as a geyser of scorching hot flame blew out Lancaster's faceplate from the inside and erupted out of his mech. Lancaster's mech collapsed into the rubble as flames continued to belch from where its faceplate had been.

Numerically, the odds were in the forces from the *Thrawn* favor, but Jeff knew he wouldn't be making it out of this one alive. He went to work, firing single shots from his damaged tri-barrel at the centipedes, taking as many as he could with him. The infantry troopers spread out behind him along the side of the wide-open area where the alien machine sat and concentrated their fire at the centipede warriors with were engaging them as if they were mothers defending their young.

****

Shannon sat in the command chair of the *Thrawn*'s bridge. His brow was creased in heavy thought as he watched the forward view screen. He had ordered Williams to call up several video feeds from the helmets of the ship's infantry troopers who were engaged with the centipedes in the heart of the city.

"Tell me someone has figured out what that *thing* is," he grunted, gesturing at the massive, tringle-shaped, alien machine in the heart of the city.

Lieutenant Edmond Gray, who was the ship's science officer and back-up tactical officer, was who answered him. Gray had been studying the odd radiological reading the *Thrawn*'s sensors had been picking up since they had first become aware of them.

"Whatever its purpose may be, I can tell you this, sir," Gray said. "That thing extends into the core of Cerebus VI. I believe a good portion of its power is being siphoned directly from Cerebus VI's core. It's building up, too. The power isn't being expended so much as collected."

Shannon scowled at Gray. "You're going to have to better than that, soldier."

Gray swallowed hard. "It might be these aliens version of a planet-killer weapon," he suggested weakly.

Shannon shook his head. "That just doesn't make any sense. These centipedes show up out of the blue, declare war on this system, and take the planet only to destroy it? No way. I ain't buying that. Even the most warlike races the Solar Federation has encountered over the centuries aren't that crazy. If they wanted to destroy the planet, their two super dreadnoughts could have just hammered the planet's colony to dust from orbit. There's something else going on here."

"As you say, sir." Gray shrugged. "Regardless of what it's true purpose may be, this planet will not survive it coming fully online. Of that, I can assure you."

"You're saying we need to get clear of the planet?" Shannon asked with wry, bitter smirk.

Gray nodded. "I would advise doing so as soon as possible, Captain. We have no means knowing when that thing will reach the power levels it needs to become fully functional."

"We need to leave now, sir," Shannon's XO, Williams, intruded on their conversation.

"Quiet," Shannon ordered Williams with a gesture that clearly said shut the hell up.

"Do we have time to recall our troops out there?" Shannon nodded at the forward view screen that was still streaming live feeds from several of the ship's infantry troopers.

With a great sadness in his expression, Gray shook his head. "You would be risking this ship by doing so, sir, and every onboard her."

"Cerebus VI is lost, Captain," Williams butted in again. "There's nothing we can do here but die ourselves. Admiral Early and the rest of Taskforce *need* us. We can do a lot more good up there in space than we can than sitting here waiting on Cerebus VI to go boom."

Shannon was about to come down hard on Williams, but surprisingly, the *Thrawn*'s helmsman, Redder, spoke up too. "I hate to say it, Captain, but for once, I think the newbie is right."

Williams shot an angry glare at Redder in spite of his support. On a sane ship of the Solar Federation Navy, one did not call a superior officer a newbie without consequence. The *Thrawn* was far from being a normal ship, though. Shannon's informal attitude towards his crew and treatment of them bred such insults as the one Redder had just given him. It irked Williams to no end, but the *Thrawn* belonged to Shannon. If he lived through this mess, Williams promised himself he was going to take his issues with Shannon's style of command all the way to the head of the Federation council if he had to. Something had to be done about it before the Federation Navy lost the ship from Shannon's incompetence as her captain.

"Okay then," Shannon said, leaning back deeper into his command chair. "I guess we don't have a choice. Redder, fire up the engines and get us the hell out of here."

"Yes sir," Redder barked, whirling his chair around to go to work.

Shannon took a last, sad look at the live helmet feeds from his men were who still out there battling in the heart of the city. "Get those images off the screen," he ordered.

The forward screen shifted back to a view of the lit-up night sky of Cerebus VI as Shannon buried his face in hands to give those he was leaving behind a moment of thought and silence.

****

Admiral Early clutched the arms of her command chair in a death grip as the *Castle* shook again. The massive Solar Federation super dreadnought had just taken a third round of missiles to her forward hull, adding to the damage there. The *Castle* was venting atmosphere on several decks, and her hull integrity was dangerously compromised. Admiral Early imagined what the front of the giant ship had to look like: a jagged, nearly shredded mess of carbon scars, holes, and torn metal. The *Castle* was barely holding together and couldn't take too many more hits before she broke apart.

The other ships of Taskforce Hammer weren't faring much better. There were four battleships still in the fight though the *Freedom* was barely hanging on. She'd taken the brunt of the fire when the alien battleships closed in. The *Freedom* was venting more than atmosphere. Raw energy from engines leaked into space from her jump drive. The *Chapman* and the *Taylor* had taken a beating as well. Both of them were without shields and relying on luck and evasive maneuvers. The *Rann* had lost some of her speed and overall power, but she continued to show the aliens that Federation vessels had teeth.

Taskforce Hammer's two destroyers were gone. They had died in the initial volleys of the battle that was now raging around Cerebus VI. Missiles had overwhelmed their point defense guns and ECMs, battering them into nothing more than bits of space debris.

The ships of the alien fleet and Taskforce Hammer were now intermixed and locked in close combat. The *Chapman* broke hard to port, avoiding a volley of incoming missiles even as she fired her forward railguns. Their fire raked over the side of an alien destroyer that had already taken damage digging holes into and through its hull and armor. The destroyer veered away from the *Chapman*, trying to escape her guns only to enter the path of the *Taylor*. A volley of missiles slid from the *Taylor*'s launchers to strike the destroyer head on. Its forward section exploded into a fiery mess of jagged and twisted metal. The destroyer spun onward passed the *Taylor* to plunge into an approaching alien battleship. The two of them died together.

The *Rann* was occupied by a trio of alien battleships that blocked its path. Energy rippled over their hulls and danced among the scattered spikes there before being released in bolts of pure destructive force at the *Rann*. The *Rann*'s shields held as she returned fire. Her two primary energy cannons concentrated their beams on the middle battleship. Its shields gave way as they sliced into its hull. The *Rann* shot forward, pressing its advantage over the stricken alien warship. Her side railguns opened up on the alien battleships at her flanks. One of them was gutted as the *Rann* darted passed it. The wounded ship reeled in space, breaking from its original heading, to twist sideways, leaking atmosphere. The other battleship's shields pulse beneath the hammering the *Rann*'s railguns poured onto it. It held its ground as its launchers put salvo after salvo of missiles in the void. The missiles chased after the *Rann* as she continued towards the middle alien battleship. Her energy cannons cut the battleship from bow to stern as she soared over it. Its two pieces drifted apart in space behind her.

The *Freedom*'s captain must have known his ship was dead. The Federation battleship built up what speed it could as she plunged towards a trio of alien destroyers. The lesser alien vessels poured fire into her as she approached. Entire sections of the *Freedom* were ripped away from her central mass, but she reached the destroyers, smashing herself into the closest of them. Her weakened body folded inward on itself against the armor of the destroyer's hull, but then her main drive either ruptured or was detonated by her crew. The ensuing blast finished the destroyer she had rammed and sent shockwaves of force battering the other two.

The *Chapman* and the *Taylor* formed up on each other, flying side by side, as they charged the main body of remaining alien warships. Between their combined firepower, another two alien destroyers and a battleship were sent back to whatever hell they had emerged from. The alien fleet's main body separated as the two Federation battleships continued on course for it. Fire from five battleships and six destroyers lanced outward at the *Chapman* and the *Taylor*. Missiles slammed into the *Taylor's* side as she came hard about changing her course at the last moment. Orange and white orbs of fire and heat blossomed along her length where the missiles made contact. The *Chapman* was luckier. Breaking in the other direction, her engines at full, her point defense weapons laid waste to the missiles that came streaking in at her. Two of the alien battleships lunged after her in pursuit, their beam weapons lashing outward to cut deep groves into her aft sections. The damage looked worse than it was. The *Taylor*, however, had been shaken to her core by the impact of the alien missiles. Like a wounded man limping along on one leg, she brought herself around again to face the alien warships. The forward weapons dealt vengeance upon the closest of them. Her railguns gutted the underside of the alien battleship she fired on.

It disappeared in a flash of light and flame as her railguns continued to fire.

An alien destroyer came blazing towards the *Taylor*. It was battle damaged but not out of the game. Energy bolts whipped outwards from its forwards spikes to sever the *Taylor* at mid-ship. The two halves of the *Taylor* drifted away from each other as if in slow motion before the erupted in flames and blew completely apart.

Admiral Early took stock of the situation. There were twelve remaining alien battleships and fifteen alien destroyers still engaged with the ships under her command. All in all, Taskforce Hammer had pulled off a miracle doing as much as it had to the alien fleet, but it wasn't enough. They remained greatly outnumbered and outgunned since her super dreadnought flagship, the *Castle*, had lost most of its weapon systems. She had to order a retreat before it, along with the *Chapman* and the *Rann*, were lost as well. The thought of retreating gnawed at her. She wasn't one to give up even when the odds were against her. She was the sort who kept on fighting until either she or her enemies were dead. As the commanding officer of Taskforce Hammer, though, Admiral Early knew she had a lot more to consider than just her personal sense of honor.

"Admiral!" her XO yelled at her. "We're picking up some very strange readings from the planet!"

Now is not the time, she wanted to scream at her XO, but she bit her tongue and merely snapped, "Report!"

"The strange energy readings we've been monitoring have grown in power beyond anything we've ever encountered short of a planet-killer style weapon, ma'am!"

"Are you saying the planet could explode?" Admiral Early whirled towards her XO, her eyes wide.

"Exactly, ma'am!" he confirmed. "We need to get clear of it ASAP!"

"Admiral!" her sensor tech called for her attention. "We've got company!"

"Onscreen!" Admiral Early ordered, half-expecting to see more alien warship jumping into the system. Instead, she saw the *Thrawn* rising out of Cerebus VI's atmosphere like a hellhound with its teeth bared.

The *Thrawn*'s weapon systems lit up the darkness of the void around Cerebus VI as she let loose on the alien warships that were still engaging Taskforce Hammer. One alien battleship died as wave after wave of heavy missiles smashed its shields and punched holes in its armor. Another was sliced and diced by the *Thrawn*'s railguns as they utterly shredded it. Still another alien battleship suffered the wrath of the *Thrawn*'s forward energy cannons. One second, its shields flashed, and the next, the entire battleship was turned into an exploding mess of debris and alien corpses.

"Been keeping busy I see," Admiral Early heard Captain Shannon's voice laughing over the fleet-wide channel. "Do I always have to drag that cute bottom of yours out of the fire, Samantha?"

Admiral Samantha Early didn't know whether to shed tears of joy or order her gunners to open fire on Shannon for his snide remarks. In the end, she settled for ignoring his comment for now and promising herself he would bleed later.

"Captain Shannon!" she exclaimed. "Welcome back to the fight!"

"I never left it, Sam," he said grimly, his words drenched in pain. "I had to leave hundreds of good men and women down there to die."

Admiral Samantha Early was taken aback by the sincerity and level of hurt that had suddenly come over Shannon.

"Any idea what that thing powering up down there is?" she asked.

"None whatsoever," Shannon told her. "I suggest we get as far away from it as we can, though."

"All ships, form up on the *Thrawn*," Admiral Early ordered over the fleet-wide channel. "She's going to lead us out of here."

"With pleasure," Shannon said, and she could imagine the lopsided smile that must be stretched across his lips as he spoke.

****

The sudden appearance of the *Thrawn* had changed the course of the battle. The massive near super dreadnought class vessel's fire had scattered the alien warships into complete disarray and taken out three of their twelve battleships with its opening volley. Losing a fourth of their battleships so quickly had put the alien warships on the defensive. Shannon knew it wouldn't be long until they got their act together, though. They were already attempting to do so as the smaller groups they had split up into gave chase to Taskforce Hammer.

Taskforce Hammer's speed was greatly reduced by Admiral Early's super dreadnought, the *Castle*. The massive super dreadnought had never been designed for speed anyway, and now with all the damage it had taken since entering the Cerebus system, it was limping along at a snail's pace compared to the other ships of the taskforce. Shannon had no intention of leaving it behind, however, and not just because Samantha was its commanding officer. The super dreadnought's crew numbered in the thousands, and after leaving so many of his men to die on the surface of Cerebus VI, Shannon wasn't about to leave anyone else behind if he could help it.

The *Thrawn* had taken up position in the rear of the retreating forces of the taskforce behind the *Castle*. Her point defense and electronic counter-measures were being pushed to the limit as they strained to protect both her and the super dreadnought. Shannon refused to give up the fight. The *Thrawn*'s aft weapon systems spat what missiles they could towards the alien warships. She was far from being defenseless against the aliens behind her, but she was built to go charging in, not to cover a retreat.

The aliens' numerical advantage kept most of the *Thrawn*'s missiles from reaching their targets as the alien warships closed in on one another overlapping their screens of defense and merging their shields where and when they could.

Alarm klaxons were blaring throughout the *Thrawn* as fire from the alien warships continued to pound into her aft sections and topside. So far, the damage was minimal, but that, too, wouldn't last. The *Thrawn* was a tough ship, but even she wasn't indestructible. The aliens were wearing her down. Shannon considered bringing her about and engaging the remaining alien ships head on. Even as outnumbered as she was, the *Thrawn* could easily do a great a deal damage to the alien warships and still be able to punch through the line they were forming and escape. If he did that, though, it would leave the *Castle*, the *Rann*, and the *Chapman* on their own without the *Thrawn* to defend them. He figured the *Rann* might survive, given that she was mostly undamaged and her captain was clearly very good at her job. The *Chapman* and the *Castle* wouldn't stand a chance, though. They would be overrun and destroyed before he could ever maneuver the *Thrawn* around again to come to their aid. No, his only choice was to keep taking a beating and hope that *Thrawn* held out long enough for Admiral Early to come up with a plan better than anything he could think of. Shannon often had moments of genius when it came to space battles and was a competent ship captain, but his real strengths lay more in the offensive direction. He was very good at killing in general, but his skill set was better suited to being a ground commander than a naval one. Samantha Early he knew was among the best of the best, not *the* best, ship officer the Solar Federation Navy had ever produced.

Shannon started to order a channel opened to the *Castle* when things took a very nasty turn for everyone. Cerebus VI shuddered in space, waves of disrupted space-time hurling outward from it. Shannon snapped at his bridge crew to get an image of the planet on the bridge's forward screen even has his science officer was yelling to him about the state of the planet. An image of Cerebus VI appeared on the forward screen as the waves already emanating caught up to the alien ships behind Taskforce Hammer. They were tossed about like the toys of an angry child in space. All of them were knocked off course, with some of them even spinning end over end. The waves proved too much for four of the alien destroyers and one of the surviving battleships that was too damaged to hold up against them. Those ships died in fiery blasts that flashed like old Earth fireworks behind the *Thrawn.*

"Brace for impact!" Shannon howled at the top of his lungs. "All available power to shields!"

The waves hit the *Thrawn* like a wedge being forced suddenly under her. She was tossed upwards. Her inertial dampers did their best to minimize the impact of what got through her shields, but even so, she took a beating. Crewmen were flung about the bridge like ragdolls as several stations shorted out in erupting explosions of sparks and flames. Shannon clutched the arms of his command chair, gritting his teeth while knowing he was helpless to stop the chaos unfolding around him. Then it was all over as soon as it had begun. The waves raced onward towards the other ships ahead of the *Thrawn.* Only then did Shannon notice the image on the bridge's forward view screen. Cerebus VI was gone. In its place was a giant hole in space itself. Through it, the stars were different and strange. At least the portion of the stars that Shannon could see. Most of what he could see through the hole in space was more alien warships like those who had shown up out of the blue to attack Cerebus VI. Not even the AI of the *Thrawn* main computer could give an accurate estimate on their number. They bloated out the alien stars with the sheer mass of their armada.

"God in heaven, help us," Shannon breathed.

The waves of disrupted space-time struck the *Castle* after battering the *Thrawn*. The massive Federation super dreadnought blew apart, all of its debris and bits being swept forward by the waves as they continued onward. Admiral Samantha Early and her entire crew died instantly. The *Chapman* perished as well. The wounded battleship broke apart the second the waves struck it just as the *Castle* had. The *Rann* survived, if only barely. Her shields were nowhere near as strong as the *Thrawn*'s, nor did she have the giant carrier's mass to aid her. The waves ravaged her, tearing creases in her hull and knocking her sideways in space. She held together but appeared to be powerless and drifting with her engines off-line in the wave's wake.

Shannon stared at the image of the alien fleet as its lead ships began to move through the hole in space that had once been Cerebus VI. They entered the system in groups of twenty at a time. He counted over a dozen super dreadnoughts in those initial groups alone. There was no question in his mind that it was time to cut losses and run, but instead of doing so, he froze. His rational mind informed him that Samantha was dead, but the rest of him resisted that it of knowledge to the point that he simply locked down.

"Captain!" Williams shouted at him from what seemed like very far away. Shannon barely heard the words his XO was screaming at him. He turned his head about, his eyes taking in the damage the space-times waves had done to the bridge. Shannon saw an ensign, motionless on the deck, with half her face burnt away and a medic kneeling by her side. He stared at the charred, almost melted away part of her face and wondered if that was what Samantha must have looked like before the explosion of the *Castle* consumed her entirely.

Shannon's head snapped about as William's fist made contact with his jaw. His XO's features came into focus in front of him as Shannon lunged from his command chair to tackle Williams. He took his XO to the floor beneath him, pummeling Williams with a flurry of enraged, expertly placed blow. Teeth and blood flew from Williams' mouth as the man tried to scream, but all that came out were grunts of pain and spraying geysers of wet red.

It took Redder and another crewman to haul him off of Williams.

"Captain!" Redder wailed in his ear while doing his best to restrain Shannon's right arm while the other crewman tried to hold his left. "Shannon! You've got to snap out of it, sir!"

Redder using the word "sir" did the trick. Shannon woke up as if from a trance. Williams' beaten and crumpled body rested on the deck at his feet. He could see the XO was still breathing.

120

Shannon raised his hands up to look at the slick, redness of Williams' blood dripping from them.

He quickly pulled himself together, wiping his hands as clean as he could on the pants of his uniform. "Redder, plot us a jump out of here. Now!"

"Yes, sir!" Redder shouted, diving back into his seat at the ship's helm. "I'm on it!"

The alien warships were continuing to flood the Cerebus system. Their outlying elements had sighted the *Thrawn* and the *Rann* and were beginning to stream towards them in unimaginable numbers.

Shannon knew there was no time to evacuate the crew of the *Rann* onto the *Thrawn*. That left him with only one option, as he couldn't chance the *Rann* falling into the aliens' hands. They already seemed to know too much about the Solar Federation as it was.

"Lock forward railguns onto the *Rann*," Shannon ordered his weapons officer as a sadness fell over the bridge.

"Target acquired."

"Fire!" Shannon said flinching at the sound of his own voice.

The *Thrawn*'s railguns blazed away at the wounded, Federation battleship, until the *Rann* was nothing more than crushed and shredded debris.

"Jump plotted!" Redder yelled.

"Then get us out of here, man!" Shannon ordered.

A jump point formed in front of the *Thrawn*, and she entered it with her engines hurling her forward at maximum power.

Epilogue

Shannon waited outside the conference room. Its door was locked and four heavily armed guards stood between him at. Two whole days had passed since the battle in the Cerebus system. His ship, the *Thrawn*, had been docked for hurried repairs. All of the Solar Federation was in a panic, preparing for a war that would likely be fought to protect its very existence.

There had been a good deal of time to think since the battle, and he had used it trying to figure out just what had happened in the Cerebus system and why. He was the only surviving ship captain to emerge from the system after the battle that had been fought there. That was why he was here now, waiting for the members of the Solar Federation Council to debrief him officially. He knew they were going to pick his mind for every scrap of information he had about the aliens he had engaged there in the hopes that they could learn something, anything new about the aliens that might give them a better means of combatting them.

Shannon had heard that the aliens' massive fleet hadn't moved out of the Cerebus system yet. It had, however, dispatched smaller groups of ships to strike at the closest Federation colonies to Cerebus. Those battles were raging even now and already pushing the Solar Federation Navy to its limits. Having been the greatest power in known space for centuries, the Solar Federation found itself suddenly facing an enemy with a fleet that outnumbered its own by at least twenty to one according to even the most conservative estimates.

Frowning as he waited, Shannon believed he had finally figured out why the aliens had attacked the Cerebus system. It was the perfect strategic foothold to establish in Federation space. The Cerebus system was far enough out that the Solar Federation Navy hadn't had the forces to take it back before the aliens' secured it, and it was placed within reasonable striking distance of several other Federation systems. Having looked over the data on the aliens' initial incursion numerous times, Shannon had deduced that the first alien fleet must have been traveling through jump space for years to reach Cerebus. The ships in that first wave were rougher and not up to par with the ones that had emerged from the massive jump point the aliens had turned Cerebus VI into. It must have been their plan to take the planet and use it for that purpose from the beginning. The destruction of Cerebus VI provided them with the power to open the largest and most far-reaching jump point ever known to exist, and through it, they had put themselves into place to challenge the Solar Federation for this section of the galaxy.

The door to the conference room opened, and the guards stepped aside as Admiral Perron emerged from it. The middle-aged man marched up to Shannon, extending his hand.

"Sorry about your loss, son," Admiral Perron told him. "I knew Admiral Early very well myself. She and her talent will be missed."

"Thank you, sir." Shannon nodded politely. "But I think we've all got a great deal of losses ahead of us."

Shannon followed Admiral Perron into the room where the council awaited them as he swore inwardly that Admiral Samantha Early and all those who died in the Cerebus system would be avenged.

Read on for a free sample of The Lost Empire

Eric S. Brown is author of numerous series including the Bigfoot War series, the Crypto-Squad series (with Jason Brannon), the Kaiju Apocalypse series (with Jason Cordova), The Home world series, The "A Pack of Wolves" series, and the Jack Bunny Bam-Bam series. Some of his stand alone books include Kraken, Megalodon, Megalodons, Megalodon Apocalypse, War of the World Plus Blood Guts and Zombies, Sasquatch Lake, Crawlers, Season of Rot, and Kaiju Armageddon to name only a few. His short fiction has been published hundreds of times in the small press and beyond including markets like Baen Books' Onward Drake and Black Tide Rising anthologies, the Grantville Gazette, Walmart World Magazine, and the SNAFU anthology series. He has written the novelizations for such films as Boggy Creek: The Legend is True and The Bloody Rage of Bigfoot. Two of his own books have been adapted into feature films the first of which was Bigfoot War in 2014 by Origin Releasing. Eric also writes an ongoing comic book news column entitled "Comics in a Flash." He lives in North Carolina with his wife and two children where he continues to write tales of blazing guns, hungry corpses, and the monsters that lurk in the woods.

TASKFORCE

CHECK OUT OTHER GREAT SCIENCE FICTION BOOKS

FURNACE
by Joseph Williams

On a routine escort mission to a human colony, Lieutenant Michael Chalmers is pulled out of hyper-sleep a month early. The RSA Rockne Hummel is well off course and—as the ship's navigator—it's up to him to figure out why. It's supposed to be a simple fix, but when he attempts to identify their position in the known universe, nothing registers on his scans. The vessel has catapulted beyond the reach of starlight by at least a hundred trillion light-years. Then a planetary-mass object materializes behind them. It's burning brightly even without a star to heat it. Hundreds of damaged ships are locked in its orbit. The crew discovers there are no life-signs aboard any of them. As system failures sweep through the Hummel, neither Chalmers nor the pilot can prevent the vessel from crashing into the surface near a mysterious ancient city. And that's where the real nightmare begins.

LUNA
by Rick Chesler

On the threshold of opening the moon to tourist excursions, a private space firm owned by a visionary billionaire takes a team of non-astronauts to the lunar surface. To address concerns that the moon's barren rock may not hold long-term allure for an uber-wealthy clientele, the company's charismatic owner reveals to the group the ultimate discovery: life on the moon.

But what is initially a triumphant and world-changing moment soon gives way to unrelenting terror as the team experiences firsthand that despite their technological prowess, the moon still holds many secrets.

CHECK OUT OTHER GREAT SCIENCE FICTION BOOKS

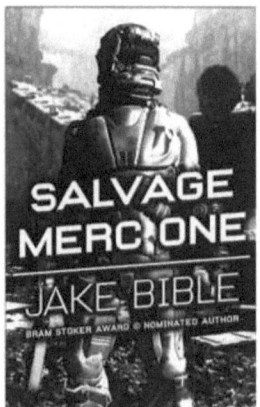

SALVAGE MERC ONE
by **Jake Bible**

Joseph Laribeau was born to be a Marine in the Galactic Fleet. He was born to fight the alien enemies known as the Skrang Alliance and travel the galaxy doing his duty as a Marine Sergeant. But when the War ended and Joe found himself medically discharged, the best job ever was over and he never thought he'd find his way again.

Then a beautiful alien walked into his life and offered him a chance at something even greater than the Fleet, a chance to serve with the Salvage Merc Corp.

Now known as Salvage Merc One Eighty-Four, Joe Laribeau is given the ultimate assignment by the SMC bosses. To his surprise it is neither a military nor a corporate salvage. Rather, Joe has to risk his life for one of his own. He has to find and bring back the legend that started the Corp.

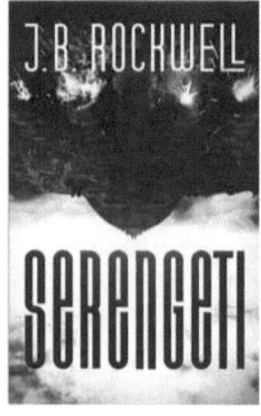

SERENGETI
by **J.B. Rockwell**

It was supposed to be an easy job: find the Dark Star Revolution Starships, destroy them, and go home. But a booby-trapped vessel decimates the Meridian Alliance fleet, leaving Serengeti—a Valkyrie class warship with a sentient AI brain—on her own; wrecked and abandoned in an empty expanse of space. On the edge of total failure, Serengeti thinks only of her crew. She herds the survivors into a lifeboat, intending to sling them into space. But the escape pod sticks in her belly, locking the cryogenically frozen crew inside.

Then a scavenger ship arrives to pick Serengeti's bones clean. Her engines dead, her guns long silenced, Serengeti and her last two robots must find a way to fight the scavengers off and save the crew trapped inside her.

CHECK OUT OTHER GREAT SCIENCE FICTION BOOKS

MAUSOLEUM 2069
by **Rick Jones**

Political dignitaries including the President of the Federation gather for a ceremony onboard Mausoleum 2069. But when a cloud of interstellar dust passes through the galaxy and eclipses Earth, the tenants within the walls of Mausoleum 2069 are reborn and the undead begin to rise. As the struggle between life and death onboard the mausoleum develops, Eriq Wyman, a one-time member of a Special ops team called the Force Elite, is given the task to lead the President to the safety of Earth. But is Earth like Mausoleum 2069? A landscape of the living dead? Has the war of the Apocalypse finally begun? With so many questions there is only one certainty: in space there is nowhere to run and nowhere to hide.

RED CARBON
by D.J. Goodman

Diamonds have been discovered on Mars.

After years of neglect to space programs around the world, a ruthless corporation has made it to the Red Planet first, establishing their own mining operation with its own rules and laws, its own class system, and little oversight from Earth. Conditions are harsh, but its people have learned how to make the Martian colony home.

But something has gone catastrophically wrong on Earth. As the colony leaders try to cover it up, hacker Leah Hartnup is getting suspicious. Her boundless curiosity will lead her to a horrifying truth: they are cut off, possibly forever. There are no more supplies coming. There will be no more support. There is no more mission to accomplish. All that's left is one goal: survival.

CHECK OUT OTHER GREAT SCIENCE FICTION BOOKS

IN PERPETUITY
by Jake Bible

For two thousand years, Earth and her many colonies across the galaxy have fought against the Estelian menace. Having faced overwhelming losses, the CSC has instituted the largest military draft ever, conscripting millions into the battle against the aliens. Major Bartram North has been tasked with the unenviable task of coordinating the military education of hundreds of thousands of recruits and turning them into troops ready to fight and die for the cause.

As Major North struggles to maintain a training pace that the CSC insists upon, he realizes something isn't right on the Perpetuity. But before he can investigate, the station dissolves into madness brought on by the physical booster known as pharma. Unfortunately for Major North, that is not the only nightmare he faces- an armada of Estelian warships is on the edge of the solar system and headed right for Earth!

BATTLEFIELD MARS
by David Robbins

Several centuries into the future, Earth has established three colonies on Mars. No indigenous life has been discovered, and humankind looks forward to making the Red Planet their own.

Then 'something' emerges out of a long-extinct volcano and doesn't like what the humans are doing.

Captain Archard Rahn, United Nations Interplanetary Corps, tries to stem the rising tide of slaughter. But the Martians are more than they seem, and it isn't long before Mars erupts in all-out war.